NIGHT OF THE
FURIES

A NEW PULP PRESS BOOK

First New Pulp Press Printing, November 2013

This book is a work of fiction. Names, characters, places, and
incidents either are the products of the author's imagination or are
used fictitiously, and any resemblance to actual events or persons,
living or dead, is entirely coincidental.

ISBN-13: 978-0-9855786-9-5

ISBN-10: 0-9855786-9-6

Printed in the United States of America

Visit us on the web at www.newpulppress.com

To Rory

NIGHT OF THE
FURIES

J.M. TAYLOR

Opening Statement

Killing my mother was easy. It wasn't the first time I've killed, and it probably won't be the last.

It's not like she was a saint. She didn't even know me. Who'd have sympathy for a mother that didn't know her own kid? But like I said, it wasn't my first time taking a life.

When she stepped into the bedroom at the top of the stairs, I was already waiting for her. She didn't recognize me at first. How's that for a greeting after thirty years? But when I showed her the birthmark, my one lock of white hair that still stood out against the grays coming in, she knew, and she knew why I was there. It was her own people who said there's always a price for betrayal, that fate will step in and punish you for killing your husband. I was Fate's hit man.

So, when I shot her and that pansy ass lover of hers, she got exactly what she deserved, and she couldn't do a damn thing but accept it.

"What are you going to do?" she said. "Shoot your own mother? The one who gave you life?"

"The day you killed my father, you took my life."

She denied it, of course. That song and dance about having nothing to do with it. But when the weak old man walked in, the one who'd taken my father's place, he knew right away. I could see it in his eyes. "No," he said. "You can't be here."

"You never see someone for the last time," I told him. "Not until they're dead." I didn't give him a chance to say anything else. I squeezed the trigger, twice, and he went down. I watched him gasping on the floor of the short hallway at the top of the stairs. He tried to stand, clutching at the end of the banister, but his bloody hand slipped, and he fell backwards, halfway down the stairs. The sound of the shots echoed off the walls.

She watched him go down. When his body got hung up, one leg stuck in the railing, she sniffed, raised her chin, then faced me as if nothing had happened. The heartless bitch. She stood there, bold as brass, but then I shot her, too. She took two staggering steps back. For a second I thought I was going to have to waste another bullet on her, but then her whole body seemed to raise up, then floated in mid-air before she fell down on top of him. The impact loosened his leg, and the two of them skidded the rest of the way down to the landing. I had to kick at his arm to get by them.

When I walked out into the night, the cool summer air washed over me, and for the first time in over thirty years, I felt the weight off my soul. I had avenged my father, as any good son would. I tucked the gun, a four-inch Colt Python, into my pants and made my way down the street, covering the three blocks calmly, but briskly. I heard the sirens just as I was getting into the stolen Olds I'd stashed in the public lot. It seemed like a long walk, but I cut across the tracks and stayed mostly out of sight. I put on an old man's slouch hat, pulled it down low, and drove slowly to the highway. I passed a pair of cop cars and an ambulance speeding to the scene as I crossed the intersection onto Route 1 heading south. They'd be too late.

Chapter 1
Summer 1967

I've been on the road a half hour, and now I'm about to cross into Rhode Island. I just heard a radio report saying that Peter "Bricks" Mancini, reputed mob boss of Boston, has been killed, along with his wife. They're already saying it was a hit by another crime family, either a local hit or from New York. Idiots. If they only knew how little it mattered to me whether Mancini had lived or died. And I couldn't care less about the other families. I just wanted to kill that faithless old woman, and the world is better off without her.

The sound of the motor and wheels eating up the road drown out the radio. I turn it up, and the voices rattle in my brain. I hear only scattered words, like, "rose through the ranks from the slums of Boston," and "ruthless killer," and "You're a ghost." No, that's *her* voice. I turn up the radio as far as it will go, roll down the windows until the wind whips off my old man hat and carries it into the darkness, but still I can hear her.

It won't be for long, though. I should reach New York before dawn, and I can ditch this Delta and get another car, and then disappear. As long as I keep moving, as long as I keep putting distance between me and her, as long as I keep this wind howling in my ears, then I won't have to listen to her.

"I never betrayed a soul," she said.

Like hell.

"If I made your life hard, it was because he was never there to make it easy. I raised you alone."

She has — had — no idea what the truth was. But I do. He told me.

How many times did he take me for long walks through the neighborhood, teaching me about life? He'd show me the tall houses where the rich bastards lived, and told me how they'd climbed up those high steps on the backs of people like him. Then, at the end of the next block, he'd point out a group of losers huddled around a trash can fire. "Don't be those bums, Giorgio," he'd tell me. "Do something with your life, and don't let those rich bastards take it way from you."

Once, he took me to see Jimmy Smiles, the guy that gave him start. By this time, the old man was long out of the racket, but his old friends came around every day to make sure he was doing all right. It was a summer day, when I was maybe six or seven. Jimmy sat in a kitchen chair on the sidewalk outside the barbershop where he'd held court for so long. He had a ripped, stained hat on top of his bald head, his smile more like a skeleton's leer. They talked about the news on the street, and my father asked his opinion on some deal he was making. Jimmy mumbled a few words that I barely understood, but my father nodded like he was listening to the Oracle at Delphi in the stories my mother used to tell me. Then I saw my father slip a few bucks in Jimmy's tattered shirt pocket, like he was still paying protection. Jimmy patted my head and kept mumbling, even as we walked away.

"What'd you think of that?" he asked me when were out of earshot of Jimmy.

"It didn't make any sense to me," I said.

"I didn't ask about that, numbskull. Do you really think I needed his help?"

I was confused, but tried not to show it. I figured there

was something I should've gotten out of that visit, but for the life of me I couldn't see it. Finally, Papa told me.

"See, guys like that, they never realize when their time's up. Old Jimmy barely knows his name some days, but he remembers he used to be a big shot around here. And he was. I owe him half of what I got, and that means you owe him, too. So every few days, I stop by, shoot the breeze, and give his tribute money. Between me and a few other guys, we pay his rent and groceries. That's what you do. That's being a man."

Did my mother ever teach me a thing like that? Like hell she did. Pay attention.

Chapter 2

1927

I was ten the year my father died. Back then, we lived in East Boston, on Putnam Street. The tenements were shoved up close to each other, and the noise went on all day and night. We had an apartment on the third floor, above the couple that owned the bakery on the first floor. It was just the three of us, but you'd never know it the way people were always coming and going.

Most Fridays, my father's friends came over to play pinochle or poker till late in the night. When they showed up, my mother made pots of spaghetti and what seemed like gallons of tomato sauce. All those guys — Al, Carmine, and that turncoat Mancini — were big men, and when they played cards, they liked to eat their fill, too. They sat at a big table in the front room. I always thought it was funny that they played only for pennies, or maybe, sometimes, nickels. Papa brought jugs of wine from under the bed or the back of the closet. The jugs always needed to be refilled the next morning.

The smell of cigars reached me across two rooms and through a closed door. Even though they spoke loudly, I could only make out snatches of what they said. Most of it was Italian, with only a smattering of English. It was a comforting rumble, one voice melting into another. But I could pick Papa's voice out clearly, the last thing I heard before falling asleep.

And where was my mother? Card nights, she stayed out of the parlor, but never left the house, never went out to see her own friends. Instead, she'd put me to bed, then go into the kitchen and cook some more, or do her sewing or ironing. She was a good wife, because my father kept her in line.

They played deep into the morning, and when I woke up, the only sign of the game would be the dying smell of cigar smoke mixed with the rising smell of warm bread from the bakery. Whatever time the games ended, my mother cleaned up. Papa slept late. He didn't have to get up until after most people had their lunches. Because of that, I rarely saw him before I left for school.

See, my father was Rico DiGiacomo. They called him "The Gentleman," and he was a boss before any of that crew from Providence or New York came up here. You might've seen the pictures of him in the old gangster books if you're into that stuff. You can even see that bit of white hair over his forehead, the same one I've got.

He got his start selling fruit in 1916. He had a homemade cart built on a borrowed five dollars and stocked with bananas starting to turn brown. Two years later, he'd earned enough to justify a second cart, which his friend Carmine Andreotti built and pushed. Together they split the western side of East Boston, along Bennington Street, where the streetcar led to the waterfront. They converted Carmine's basement into a banana ripening room, insulating it to retain the heat. Every morning, they took their carts onto the South Ferry and went across the harbor to the Atlantic Fruit Company in the North End.

Soon, they were selling all kinds of fruit, not just bananas. Pushing those carts, lugging crates of apples and bunches of bananas with tarantulas hiding in them, ready to attack, it was brutal work. But he did it, and without complaint. "What a man does for his family," he'd say to me.

Carmine and my father had no choice but to pay protection. They split the weekly "tax" of a dollar per cart. Otherwise, a careless boy might stumble and knock over a cart, or someone might dump a tub of bathwater at just the wrong moment and spoil the bananas. Every Friday, my father took two dollars from a cigar box he kept under his bed and delivered the cash to a man named Jimmy Smiles, who seemed to do nothing but sit in a barbershop on the corner of Brooks and Saratoga Streets reading the race results.

A year after that, in 1919, I was born, and Jimmy Smiles offered my father a piece of his policy game. He must've liked the way my father operated. Maybe the way he kept the young punks from running wild in the streets, the way he earned respect from the neighborhood. Whatever, he started selling three-digit numbers along with bananas. It was the kind of thing he handled himself, and he never told Carmine. It wasn't long after that before Jimmy Smiles was a memory and my father was calling the shots himself. He got out of the fruit business, and moved on to bigger things. Yeah, he watched out for all of us, but my mother never appreciated it.

Instead, she griped about how she'd come down in the world.

"What my people gave to the world," was her favorite line. "The Romans, they copied everything, brutes and nothing more."

"But Mama, you're Italian, too," I said, a little boy too young to know better. I was huddled against the arm of the couch, breathing through my mouth so I didn't have to smell her perfume without looking like I was trying to get away from her. I didn't know it then, but it was the perfect scent for her: like peaches, but too sweet. That's her all over.

"Sicilians aren't Italian," she said. "My blood is mostly Greek. That makes you part Greek, too, and don't forget it."

Then she'd launch in to another one of those old fairy tales, about Athena turning a girl into a spider, or how Hera, angry because her husband Zeus took a mortal lover, tricked the girl into making the god come to her as a thunderbolt. All she ever told me were stories about a woman's vengeance. She didn't think about anything else. But I did like the end of that last one, because from the fires of the girl's burning body, Zeus scooped out his son, the god Dionysus, Twice Born. Zeus finished the job of bringing him to term. Zeus was the real parent, the father who kept his boy safe.

I guess those stories were all right for a little boy, but when I was bigger, my father told me some real tales. Stories about what he did in the neighborhood, how he got to be such a big shot. Like the time he "convinced" a father who beat his daughter to apologize to her. Or the story about a dock worker, who incidentally had tried to cheat my father out of the "tax" he owed. The loser ended up bloated and unrecognizable, the waves banging his head against the hull of a docked ship. But my favorite was how he'd gotten out of the fruit business.

Exhibit for the Defense

"Listen to me, kid. This is how you deal with a pain in the ass."
We're walking down Bennington Street. People nod and wave
to my father. He walks like he's the mayor, and they show me
respect because I'm with him.

"A while back, I'm in my office in the North End. This flunky
from the biggest fruit distributor come to see me. Name me a
fruit company."

"I only heard of Sweet 'n' Fine, Papa."

"That's the one. They had almost all of the Boston market.
Except me."

"What happened?"

He hits my ear with the back of his hand. "Pay attention.
See, he walks in all nervous. Calls himself Slocumb, but he
won't look me in the eye. Never trust a guy who can't keep his
eyes in one place. They're trapped animals, liable to attack any
minute." He laughs. "It was August, and this loser's sweating right
through his seersucker suit. He had a straw hat that wilted like
old cabbage, and he kept wiping his face with a handkerchief.

"So I says to him, 'What can I do for you today, Mr. Slocomb?
Are you and Sweet 'n' Fine in such a bad way that you need
my help?' He smiled, but really he just stared at my white hair."

"Like what I have, Papa?"

"That's right, Giorgio. It's your birthmark. So this guy Slocumb says, 'Actually, Mr. DiGiacomo, I've come with a different
offer.'" My father starts talking like some nasally Midwestern,

and it makes me laugh. He looks at me angry at first, but then he decides to ham it up even more. "He says, 'Mr. DiGiacomo, I hear you're a man who likes things up front, so I'll get right to it. My company is interested in buying the business you run in East Boston. We're going to sign a contract with a large new grocery store opening in your area, and sell fruit directly to them. So we're going to buy you out.'"

"But Papa," I say, "I thought…"

He raises his hand and I shut up. "You wanna learn or not? If you're gonna take this over when I'm gone, you gotta know what you're doing. So I say to the guy, this Slocumb character, 'You want to buy my carts, eh? What about the shop I opened last month? You want that, too?' He said he was 'authorized to negotiate' with me."

I look up at him. We're coming to the end of the street, and I can smell the salt wind coming off the harbor. He sees my face and realizes I don't know what he's talking about. "That means they didn't think I had the balls to say no to him. So I say, 'What if I don't want to sell?' That, Giorgio, is negotiating.

"But he wasn't expecting that, so suddenly this guy's all business. He stops with the handkerchief. He ain't acting anymore, and I know I got him rattled. He actually leans on my desk, like he can scare me, and says I don't have a choice." Then he mimics Slocumb's mousy voice: "'Mr. DiGiacomo, we can outsell you. Our produce will be better. Within two months, you'll be out of business. We're offering you a graceful way to leave the business, and move on to other opportunities.'

"I tell him I have other opportunities anyhow. Never get tied to just one business. Remember that."

I nod wisely, like I understand what he's talking about. "So what happened, Papa?"

"Slocumb slips this piece of paper across my desk. 'This is our offer,' he says. He says it's what all my stock and equipment and whatnot is worth, plus two months' rent."

"Was it a lot?"

This time he does smack me, but not hard enough to make me cry. He glares at me, deciding if he should finish the story. I think he just wants to relive it, whether I'm listening or not. "Yeah, it was a lot of money," he says. "But you can't think about just the money. I tell him the people in my neighborhood are my friends, they'd never desert me. So I tell him to shove his piss-ant offer, and kick him out of my office."

"Then what?"

He laughs again, a deep laugh like the growl of a bear. "A week later, Sweet 'n' Fine starts shipping fruit to this new grocery store. But wouldn't you know, some of the shipments don't show up, and the ones that do get spoiled on the way from the warehouse. Then a couple of drivers suddenly quit, right in the middle of their shifts." He frowns, and says quietly, "One never came home again." But then he cheers up.

"A week later, I decide to say hello to my friend Mr. Slocumb, and I ask him how the new business is going. Turns out he has a new offer for me. Turns out DiGiacomo and Co. Fruits is worth about two grand — twice as much as before.

"Let that be a lesson, kid."

Chapter 3
Spring 1929

When I was a kid, my best friend was Tommy Costello. Italian, not Irish. I met him when I was nine or so. He was a couple years younger than me, but we did everything together, playing marbles or stickball with other kids in the neighborhood, then, later, shooting craps against an alley wall. When we got older, like when I was ten or eleven, we went over to Wood Island to dig for clams. But what really knocked Tommy out was the harbor. He couldn't get enough of watching the ships constantly sailing in and out to places unknown.

"What's the big deal?" I asked him. "Airplanes gonna take over now."

"Like hell," Tommy said. "I'd like to see a plane carry the cargo a ship does, or go half as far." That was the thing about Tommy. Always living in the past. I wanted what was new and exciting.

"They're faster," I said. "Besides, Lindy crossed the Atlantic a couple years ago."

He ignored the crack about Lindberg. "Planes are noisy. I hear them taking off all the time, and I live half a mile away from the airfield."

"You can put machine guns on an airplane and have dogfights and fly loops."

Tommy looked at me like I was crazy. "Machine guns?

Machine guns can't beat cannons." He had me there, but I liked to get him riled. You couldn't argue with Tommy when it came to nautical stuff. He memorized the names of every steamer that came into the harbor. It was a special treat for him to get two cents and take the South Ferry over to the North End. All I had to do was ask my father for the pennies, and he'd usually give me a dime to get us something to eat, too.

When we had the money, we'd walk down Louis Street to Maverick Square, past the clouds of feathers of the chicken houses and the dank stench of the wool warehouses. It was only a few minutes' sail to the North End, but Tommy soaked it up for all it was worth. He'd stand by the open windows, filling his lungs with the sea air, feeling the heave of the water and waving at the other boats we passed. Once a tug boat pilot tooted its horn, I don't even know if it was for Tommy, but I thought he was going to die and go to heaven right there.

We docked at Atlantic Avenue, and we'd weave our way through the pushcarts full of waffles, ice cream, slush, and crabs. I remember the crab sellers used to sell the ones with missing claws to the guys that were really hard up, the real losers, for only a penny.

We walked straight along Hanover Street, right through the North End. The neighborhood was a lot like Noodle Island, our name for East Boston: mostly Italian, with pastry shops and grocers on every block. But it had a completely different feel. Where we had rows of tenements lining the wide streets, with a streetcar track running down the center, the North End was dark and close. The roads were short and narrow, and you could get lost two blocks from where you started. It seemed as though people were crammed into every space, with entire families living in single rooms of every apartment, like the Black Hole of Calcutta. In East Boston, yeah, it was crowded, but you had elbow room. The North End wasn't a neighborhood, it was a holding pen.

When Tommy and me got off the docks, we jumped head-long into this mix, pushing our way down Hanover Street. There's an elevated highway that cuts it off now, but back then, the North End flowed right into the reek of meat and produce at the Quincy Market warehouses. Trucks rumbled by and men pushed carts of bananas, tomatoes, and sides of beef in a mass of confusion that never stumbled.

I liked being in the middle of it all, I liked blending in to the background and watching the world move around me, but Tommy was always on the watch for sailors. Between the Navy Yard in Charlestown and all the other ships that came in, he was never disappointed. He watched them in awe as they hustled past in their colorful uniforms, especially the navy guys in their funny hats and the bell-bottom pants that those long-haired hippies are wearing now. Tommy could tell me what rank each one was, and recognized the more exotic outfits of most of the foreign seamen. I wondered where he learned all this stuff. I mean, he was always with me.

One time, I was feeling hemmed in, excited, and I got Tommy to go a bit farther down Hanover Street, all the way to Cambridge Street, the edge of Scollay Square. I goaded him all the way to the marquee of the Old Howard theater, but that was as far as he'd go. "Let's go back," he said, tugging at my arm.

"We just got here," I said. "Let's look around." Something was always going on at Scollay Square. The sailors Tommy idolized blew all their money there. Other men escaped from the rest of the world into its convoluted alleys, sometimes never to come out again. Most of the women in the Square were a known quantity, and you could be sure there weren't many schoolteachers among them. Over the roar of the music halls and burlesque houses, you could always hear the shouting and rioting of a nonstop party. It mixed into the same kind of din as my father's card games, but without the comfort. This was a forbidding sound, threatening and evil.

I wanted to be a part of it.

Not that Tommy got scared easily. Not by a long shot. Growing up in East Boston was tough, and we both got in our share of scraps, especially with those potato-eating micks. They didn't hassle me much, on account of my father, but Tommy wasn't so lucky, and if he got jumped, that meant I got involved, too. It was usually the bigger kids, but Tommy and me gave as good as we got, and that was no mean feat. See, my father showed me how to handle myself in a street fight, but Tommy, he was pure blind fury, and when you set him off, he'd use anything handy to hurt you.

After a battle, I'd come home with a fat lip and blood all over my shirt. My mother would swear in Greek and Italian as she scrubbed the stains out so I'd have something to wear to school the next day. But my father would narrow his eyes and nod at me with approval. He taught me: want to be a better card player, sit at the table with a pro. You want to learn to fight, take on bigger kids. And if they leave you alone for a while, start something yourself, just to stay loose. Me and Tommy knew it was important to pay our dues. We wouldn't be kids forever.

That summer, there was a lot of crap happening at home, my mother pestering my father and him leaving for days at a time. When Tommy came up with the idea of building a raft, I went along because I thought it was good way to get my mind off things. We scrounged wood from trash piles and alleys, found some lengths of rope, and swiped handfuls of nails from a barrel in the hardware store. Tommy even wanted to run up a flag, so we spent a week just looking for something, anything, that would work as a mast. In the end we found a good length of pipe.

Every time we got a new piece, we stashed it in a little pile behind the ironworks on Prescott Street. You could see the orange glow of molten iron through the smoky windows, and black smoke filled the sky. The sound of giant hammers and huge machines drowned out the sound of our own childish banging. Back then, the harbor was much bigger than it is now, but they were always dumping landfill behind the works. We did our work sitting on chunks of boulders and heaps of scrap metal that were slapped and stained by the waves.

We spent hours every day pounding on bent nails with hammers we swiped from our houses. At first, it looked like we'd never get near putting our raft in the water. The boards didn't line up, and they were so thin they'd split if the nail didn't go straight.

By early June, we had something that at least looked like a raft. But one morning, we showed up to find the pieces shattered, some drifting on the brown waves. We stared at it, unbelieving.

"This is your fault," Tommy said, his lip trembling. "I told you, you didn't pull it up far enough from the water."

"Like hell. I was carrying the tools. You're the one who fucked up." He knew I was right, that he'd ruined it himself, but that changed in a second when we heard a voice jeering behind us.

"Yo-ho-ho! You little assholes sailing away to Tahiti or sompin'? Well, you'll have to do better'n that. It didn't take nothin' to wreck that piece o' shit."

We turned and saw two micks, a couple of years older than us, laughing their freckles off. Tommy didn't think, he just charged the bigger boy with a scream that surprised even me. Before I could do anything, his hammer was buried in the kid's nose. He went down, stunned, blood spraying everywhere. A second later, though, he was on top of Tommy, his fists pistoning like the hammers in the ironworks, and as much blood poured from Tommy's lip.

I knew Tommy would get his ass kicked for sure, so all I could do was go after the other one. The four of us were rolling in the dirt, the junk on the ground hurting us as much as the punches.

Even though the Irish kids were bigger and stronger than us, Tommy's fury wore his opponent out. I did OK, too. I was thinking about the shit at home, either the screaming or the silence, and for the first time in months, I felt like I was actually getting something done. It felt good when I slugged my kid in the nose, and when he fell I turned and saw Tommy on top of the other one, a sharp clump of iron in his hand, dangerously close to the kid's left eye. I saw my guy get shakily to his feet, but we were both too scared of what we saw to care about each other.

Tommy was screaming, "You fucking bastard, that was my fucking boat! If you don't fix it right fucking now, I'll pop your eye out like it was a fucking meatball!"

Like I said, we'd been in plenty of fights, and I'd seen Tommy mad before. But he never swore. Maroon blood dripped from his mouth, mixing with the sluggish ooze that still flowed from the older boy's nose. I could see murder in his eyes, and so could the micks. It flickered like the furnace in the factory, and it was something I didn't understand. In all the fights I'd been in, I never got wound up. You hit me, I hit you, that's it. Nothing emotional about it. Come to think of it, I'd never felt emotional about anything, couldn't see what the point was. Now this over a stupid boat we built for the hell of it.

The kid was blubbering, his words choking on blood. "I'm sorry! I'm fucking sorry! It was just a joke! Honest! Listen, I know where to get wood. Good shit, railroad ties in the yard across the street! You can build a real boat. Don't gouge out my eye! Fuck, I'll build it for you. Christ, just don't gouge out my fuckin' eye!"

Nobody moved for a minute, and the trapped boy started to cry, loud enough to hear over the din of the ironworks. The other one panted, "He's telling the truth. Let him go, and I promise all the shit you need will be right here when you come tomorrow. Let him go."

For a long time Tommy didn't move. The fight had gone out of the rest of us, but he still needed satisfaction. "Do something," the other kid said to me. I heard the pleading in his voice, but I felt pegged to the ground.

Finally, Tommy whispered, "I'll kill you in your sleep if you're lying. And if you're not, I still might kill you." I knew that Tommy, not even ten years old, meant every word. More importantly, so did the Irish kids.

Slowly, Tommy stood up, and the boy closed his eyes and cried. His friend helped him up, and they walked away. When they were gone, Tommy fainted. He came to after I soaked my shirt in the water and slapped his face with it. He opened his eyes and smiled. "That'll teach 'em," he said. Then he threw up.

The morning after we fought the micks, I met Tommy outside the bakery, and we made our way to the ironworks. Figuring the Irish punks would bring friends instead of wood, we each hid knives in our pockets and carried our hammers in tight grips. We were ready.

We got to the iron works, skirting around the tall fence, craning our necks to see if we were getting ambushed. "I don't see nothin'," Tommy said. He looked disappointed. Still, we snuck past the huge building, the constant crash of hammers and the roar of the furnaces covering our footsteps. We made it to the water, and the micks were nowhere in sight. But they had lived up to their promise. Stacked against a pile of twisted black scrap metal, we found three or four railroad ties, one with a spike sticking out like a knife. Behind those the kids stacked a bundle of two-by-fours, and a small wooden cask of nails. We must've scared the living shit out of them, because this stuff, except the railroad ties, was all new. They'd gone through a lot of trouble to get it, but we didn't even care to thank them, even if we ever did see them again, which we didn't. As far as Tommy was concerned, they'd gotten off easy. I could tell he still wished he'd popped that eyeball. It scared me, but I was fascinated, too. It meant we'd bought more than a boat from those shanty Irish. We'd won respect, the same way my father did it.

If nothing else, our first attempts had taught us some carpentry skills, and we were able to put the raft together in a day. We banged on those nails until our palms were blistered and bloody and our arms were weak. The wood was hard, and I bent a lot of nails trying to get them to bite into it. A few times I got my thumb, and I can still remember that sudden pain bursting up my arm.

But by the time mothers were starting to call their kids in for dinner, we had connected the ties with the two-by-fours and some broken boards left over from our first try. It was mostly straight. When they had wrecked that first raft, the micks had bent the pipe we used for the mast. Tommy and I put the angle against a boulder and tried to straighten it out. It kept turning over on us and we'd fall in heaps on the ground. We were gasping on our last try, our shirts wrapped around the pipe so we wouldn't slip on our own sweat, but it wouldn't budge. Finally, we threw it in with the rest of the scrap and put up an extra length of two-by-four instead.

That's when Tommy pulled a flag out of his pocket. It was a red triangle, all hemmed, with little tassels to tie it on. Our initials were stitched into it with white thread. After our little rumble, Tommy had to explain to his mother what we were doing, and she made it for us. I gave him ten fingers and hoisted him so he could reach the top of the mast. As he tied the flag on, he was grinning like the proud captain of a ship, and at that moment he looked every bit as happy as he had looked insane that other morning. I have to tell the truth, I almost cried.

See, this was at the same time as when my father had left for good, and my mother was on my case worse than ever. But I didn't even tell Tommy that. I knew to keep my troubles to myself, how to control my feelings. One thing I know: if you're going to kill someone, make sure you're in complete control of yourself. Otherwise, things go wrong, and you'll be in the soup for sure.

But I wasn't thinking much about that as I held Tommy so he could finish tying on the flag. "Done," he said, and I let him drop. I watched as the wind off the water picked at the flag and it snapped in the breeze. We decided to put off our maiden voyage until the next morning, when we'd have plenty of time to test her out. We walked home, tired, but too excited to take the streetcar, and Tommy told me to think up a name for the boat so we could christen it. He'd been saving pennies so he could break a bottle of tonic on the bow. He was still jabbering about it when I left him at the corner of Putnam and Lexington. I walked past the bakery to our door and went upstairs.

Exhibit for the Defense

"Listen," he'd say to me. "This is how you get rich. First, we buy the stalks of green bananas that the other guys rejected. Get them wholesale and put 'em in the ripening room." He'd rest his big hand on my shoulder, talk to me like I was one of his pals. Talk to me like we were both men.

I'd say, "Why buy them if no one else would, Papa?"

"No one could see what we could, you know what I'm saying? We'd look at those green bananas, and me and Carmine would say, yeah, we can wait 'til they're ready. Then, when the other hawkers were raising their prices, we'd pull 'em out, sell 'em for half price. Make a killing." He laughed and wagged a finger at me. "Be patient, Giorgio. Rushing only gets you trouble."

Chapter 4
Summer 1967

I'm trying to drive fast, but not too fast to catch anyone's attention. Just another car keeping steady pace on a Friday night. But that one car's been behind me at least ten minutes, even though a bunch of others have passed us both. He's hanging back there like … but no, it's too soon for that. No one would know to be looking for me. To them, I'm already dead.

I press down on the gas. The Delta's got a Super Rocket V-8, and I feel the 360 horses hauling. When I get into Providence, I'll be able to lose him. I'll have to find some way to make up the time, but what's that after thirty years of waiting? Or the two nights I spent upstairs from her bedroom, waiting like a snake to strike? It feels good to be using my legs now, to stretch out after all that lying still, being careful so they wouldn't hear me in their attic.

But I heard them. For two nights I camped out directly over their bedroom. I lay a few feet over their bed, listening to them talk about his business. She knew everything. Or at least everything he told her, and that was mostly lies.

I was less than ten feet above them, but they never suspected I was there. I was close enough to hear them get undressed, to hear the *clink* of her diamond earrings falling into a metal dish.

I heard him say, "We brought in a lotta dough this week."

I heard her say, "Then get me that fur stole."

"Anything, *cara mia*," he answered. I'll say this for her, at least she took him for all he was worth. Or maybe it was the only way he could keep her, by paying her off. Either way, how much had she gotten out of him over the years? But it didn't matter: all that money should have been mine. It was *my* father who started the racket. I should've been the one to take over when my father was ready to pass it on to me.

Through the attic floor I heard the mattress groan, along with their old-age grunts, as they climbed into bed. I stayed awake through the night, popping the last of the red pills I'd gotten from Liz. But that's another story. One thing at a time.

I've got to keep my focus. I still haven't lost that jerk and here I am coming into Providence, following 95 as it zig-zags past the railyards. I can see the dome of the State House ahead, a giant white tit. It reminds me of … Jesus, I can't think about that scene. I'll never be able to touch a woman again. No, it looks more like one of the pictures of Greek temples my mother kept in the parlor, with rows of pillars supporting the roof.

Focus, dammit. She's gone, and so are those goddamn temples. Deal with here and now.

I don't know who's in that car, but I'm going to have to do something about him quick. I pull the Colt out of my waistband. I gave my mother and old man Bricks two shots each, so I only have two left. I got a few more rounds in the back seat, but I can't reach them right now.

There's a row of gas tanks and warehouses by the water. I pull off the highway and find my way over to them, past trucks and heavy equipment, past abandoned boats up on jacks and trailers, covered with tattered tarps. The son of a bitch is following me for sure. How could anyone be on to me already? I got out of that house clean, I know I did. And if he's on to me, how many others are out there, waiting to take a shot at me?

He's doused his lights, but I can still see his car against the shadows. I make a sudden turn into the dark alley between two warehouses, jump out of the car, and run across the road to another darkened doorway.

In the few seconds before the other car turns the corner, I catch a whiff of the ocean. It's mixed with the heavy smell of gas and oil and the sludge of low tide. A couple of times, the fresh salt smell bursts through, but it's swept away again by the petroleum. I think about my father, those walks through East Boston, and know he's with me now. The air is heavy and humid, almost thick enough to chew.

The brakes screech when he sees the Delta. I thought that car would take me as far as I needed to go, but if I get out of this jam, it won't be in that hot rod. He's driving a huge black Cadillac, long and dark and comfortable. A new Eldorado, perfect for a long trip, say, to New York. I can see him, resting his arm on the door, trying to figure out what to do. He gazes in my direction, then back at my car, then behind him. He looks like a mole, poking his blind head around. I wish I could lure him out of the car, but he's trapped and he knows it. There's no way he'll get out of the car willingly, and I can't risk sneaking up on him. But I need that car.

I can't give him a second to escape. I slide out of the doorway, make two quick steps until I'm close enough to take him, and take my last two shots.

The Python's .357 rounds both hit him square, and his head shatters. Easy prey. For the third time tonight, my ears echo with gunfire. I approach the car, and the smell of blood and gunpowder drown out the scent of the ocean for a minute. My whole life, I've had those two mixed in my mind.

I look in the window at his body. His neck snapped back with the shot, but there's nothing left of his face: it's splashed across the interior of the Caddy. His right hand is still on his belly, holding a .38. He won't be needing that, so I reach over the arm that's still resting on the window and grab the gun. It's full.

I still can't figure how he made me, but it's cinch he's not the only one. If I can make it look like he finished the job, maybe I can get a head start before they clue in to the truth.

I'm in luck. The guy's about my size. Close enough, at least, to buy some time if his friends find the Delta. I push his arm in and open the door. The arm flops down, and blood drips off it like paint pooling at my feet. I can't get squeamish now, so I ignore the mess and pat him down. I find a few bullets, a money clip packed with twenties, but no wallet. Mr. Nameless is younger than me, maybe in his early thirties. Too old to make the kind of mistake he did following me into a dead end. Then again, I've had a long time to plan this. I push on his torso, and what's left of his head flops forward. Another gush of blood, and now I'm wondering if this plan is worth it.

The place is silent, except for the sound of the waves against the shore. They're short and quick, like the last breaths of a dying animal. I wrestle him out of his coat. He's uncooperative when I try to put mine on him, but he doesn't squawk when I nearly break his arm to do it. Then I bring my car alongside his so the driver doors faced each other, and drag him into the driver's seat. Even in the dark, I can see the glistening of blood all over the ground. My hands and clothes reek of it, and it's still draining out of him, covering my car, too. It'll make the scene look real enough for me to make a few extra miles.

"Sorry, fella," I say. "You're gonna have to stand in for me. But trust me, you're in good company."

Chapter 5

Summer 1929

My father was always home Sundays. He read me the funnies until I could do it myself, and then I started reading them to him. He always laughed, even if I messed up the words. My mother made a big dinner. Macaroni she made fresh the day before, sometimes a roast, especially if Papa had done well with his fruit cart that week. If we did have meat, my father let me have some of his, but my mother never gave me a piece of my own. She thought it was a waste. My father got the lion's share, and she took a small bit for herself. I was almost ten when she finally gave me my own piece, and even that was after I had begged my father for it. She put it on my plate, but she didn't look happy about it. "You're spoiling him," she said, but she couldn't say no to him. She knew better than that, at least.

After dinner, if it was nice out, my father would borrow a friend's car and we'd go for a drive. Everywhere we went, it was in someone else's car. One time I asked him why we didn't just get one of our own, and he told me, "Giorgio, why spend money for our own car, when so many friends who would be glad to have me drive theirs?" It was years before I realized the less you own, the less they can take away from you.

I remember one particular drive, the year before my father died. He and Peter, "Bricks," as he was called then, borrowed a car to take us out to the country, Woburn or something out that way, to pick apples. I called him Uncle Peter, even though he and my father were just friends. He was always coming over to play cards or something, and he acted just like a real uncle to me. I should have known better than to trust him like that.

We were all packed in the car. Uncle Peter drove, with my father sitting next to him. Tommy was with us, and I sat between him my mother in the back.

It was a nice day, some time in October of 1928. Tommy and me climbed the trees, shaking the apples to the ground. We found some windfalls that had started to ferment, and late wasps burrowed into them, coming out drunk and angry. One came after me, but it was so slow and cross-eyed that Papa was able to grab it by the wings and pinch the stinger off it.

We had a picnic, really nothing more than a few sandwiches and a hatful of apples. By the time we went home, it was starting to get dark, and I had a stomachache. Too many green apples.

When we got back to East Boston, Uncle Peter dropped off Tommy, then me and my mother. My father went along to return the car. After throwing up the unripe apples, I went to bed and fell asleep.

I have no idea how much later it was, but it was definitely that night. Papa came into my room and sat on my bed. I woke up when the smell of the cigar smoke on his clothes got too strong to bear.

"Hi, Papa," I said.

"Hi, Giorgio. Did you have a nice day?"

"Yes, Papa."

"Good. You and Tommy are good friends, huh?"

"Mostly. Sometimes we fight."

"That's not important," he said. "Good friends get into

scraps once in a while. It's good for you. What's important is that when you need him, he's there, right?"

"Yes, Papa." I was a little scared, because he never talked to me like this, let alone sat at my bed in the dark. But I was even more interested in what he was getting at, so I didn't do anything but sit up and show him I was ready to listen.

"Bricks and me are good friends," he went on. "We're building a future for you. Not like the other guys that come over here all the time." He was talking about his other card partners, Carmine and Al. I didn't call them Uncle, but usually, if I was still awake when they came over, they each gave me a half dollar.

"But listen to me," my father said. "There's different kinds of friends. Someday, Tommy might move away, and you'll make other friends. Just remember, family is always the most important. You always gotta do what you can to protect your family, even if it means turning on your friends."

"OK, Papa." I was getting sleepy again, and my stomach was still unsettled. Why did I eat so many apples? I don't even like them all that much.

"Good boy. Now go to sleep."

Not long after that things in my house started to change. Papa was home less and less, and when he was there, he and my mother fought like hell. When he was gone, my mother never showed any kind of emotion, but her eyes were always red, as if she'd just been crying. I was too afraid to ask what happened, but she wouldn't have told me anyhow. Whatever happened, it was more important than me, and I had to fend for myself.

I started skipping school, and got good at keeping the letters from the teacher out of sight. Tommy and me roamed around for hours, dodging the truant officer, hanging out with some of the bigger kids, getting into fights. We learned to play craps, and I tried to get Tommy to call me "Snake Eyes," because I thought it sounded tough, but he was smart, said it made me sound like a loser. We took up smoking cigarettes. Not long after that, I knew things were headed for trouble: when my mother caught me with a pack of Camels, she didn't do anything but give me a half-assed slap across the face. It didn't even leave a mark.

Then one day, Papa was gone. For good. He didn't even say good-bye. It was somewhere around the beginning of spring, just starting to warm up. For a while, my mother looked out the window, watching for him, but then she stopped. Just gave up, like she knew he wouldn't ever come home again. She tried to be nice to me then, but it was too late. She'd driven him away with all her nagging, and now I didn't have a father, all because of her. I've never seen anyone so selfish as her. She never thought of me, and made things so bad Papa couldn't even tell me he was leaving. No way he would've done that if it weren't for her.

That was the same time Tommy and me finished the raft. The first time we took it out, we didn't go far. Tommy didn't tell me until then that he couldn't swim. All the time he went on about those goddamn boats and sailors, and he couldn't swim a stroke! I let him make the maiden voyage by himself while I held onto the side in about two feet of water. Finally, when he was convinced it wouldn't sink, he let me in with him. We used a couple of broken boards for paddles. By the time it was getting dark, we were about twenty yards from shore, and I had to get out again and kick the boat back to shore.

We'd been going out on the raft after school for about a week. I had to get in that filthy harbor and kick to make the thing move, but Tommy ate that sailing shit up.

"Pick it up, matey," he'd yell at me. "We're going too slow."

"I'm kicking as fast as I can," I'd answer, spitting that harbor sludge at him.

"You're as slow as molasses."

"Very funny."

"Come on, Sticky. Slow as molasses."

"You come in here and kick, then."

"You know I can't swim, Sticky."

I hated it when he called me Sticky. He picked it up when he heard one of the old ladies sitting on the stoop call me that once, on account of my birthday, January 15, 1919.

My father used to tell me he knew I was destined for greatness because of the omens that occurred when I was born. It was just like in the days of the Roman emperors, he'd say. Three days before I was born, it was barely above zero, but as my mother got closer and closer to labor, it warmed up almost to the fifties. The next day, Nebraska made sure that Prohibition would be ratified. That was going to make men like my father rich. "I knew your birth was a lucky charm," he told me. "How else could you explain that the two most important events in my life took place less than a day apart?"

But the reason I was called Sticky was the most bizarre omen of all. I was born in the middle of the biggest panic Boston had seen in years. It was just before one in the afternoon, and the midwife told my mother she was still hours from giving birth. But then the sound of an explosion and gunfire erupted across the harbor. The shock forced me along. Everyone thought the Germans were attacking, and men were running in the streets carrying sticks, shovels, whatever came to hand.

Who could believe the truth? A giant tank full of molasses, right on the water in the North End, had exploded. The "gunfire" was really rivets popping off the steel plates. A tidal wave of the gunk, close to twenty feet high, crashed through the streets, leveling warehouses and homes, and almost knocked a train off the el tracks. There were bodies stuck in the shit like bugs in amber.

I was proud of my birthday, and the signs that went along

with it. When Tommy called me Sticky, he was trying to take it away from me, because nothing particular happened when he was born. That's what got me really mad — his jealousy. Right then, it just made me kick harder.

That was the day I found out what happened to my father.

Chapter 6

Summer 1929

I awoke to the sound of footsteps coming up the stairs. I thought it was Papa, finally coming home. I sat up in bed, ready to run to him, but when I heard the rap on the door, I knew it couldn't be him. Why would he knock on his own door?

My mother answered it right away, as if she had been waiting for whoever it was. I didn't budge on my bed, it squeaked so much. I wanted to hear what was going on, and couldn't risk missing a word.

I could tell from the footsteps it was a man, and after he came in, neither him or my mother said anything for what seemed like several minutes. When she did say something, she sounded out of breath. Now I know why, but back then I thought she was still a faithful wife.

"Is it over?" she said.

"Yes, it is." I couldn't believe it! The rotten bastard Bricks!

"Who did it?" my mother asked.

"It's better you don't know."

"What about us?"

"Everything's taken care of. Don't worry about nothing. You'll be fine."

It wasn't until then that my mother began to cry, but even then it was only for a second. Her husband, *my* father, was dead, and all she said was, "Well, I'm glad it's over. I couldn't wait any more. Is that so bad?"

"Not at all. You want what's best. It had to be this way."

"Where's Rico now?"

"Probably at the morgue at City Hospital. The cops'll be here soon. You'll have to identify him."

"So there's no question."

"Right."

"What about Giorgio?"

"Leave that to me," *Uncle* Peter said. "I told you, I'll take care of everything."

The room was swimming around me. Papa was dead, and I was next. She stole my father and the future he was building for me. I hated her.

I don't know what happened next. Maybe I fell asleep, maybe I passed out from holding my breath. I never heard the police come, or my mother leave. When I woke up again, it was dawn. I had survived the night, at least, but I had no idea how much time I had left. I spent the next hour making my plan. It was all the time I could afford. Once daylight came, anything could happen, and keep me from avenging my father.

I got out of bed and dressed. It was full light, and the streets were coming alive. Horses' hooves clapped against the cobblestones, and delivery trucks coughed under the clear sky. The apartment itself was quiet. My mother still wasn't up, which I thought was strange, until I heard *him* cough. I heard her say, "Hush, you'll wake the boy." Now I knew everything I'd ever need to know.

As quietly as possible I gathered some clothes and tied them inside a shirt, then sneaked out of the house. I ran to Tommy's house and called him from the street. His mother stuck her head out the window and waved to me. Before she pulled herself back inside, Tommy was next to me, waving back at her. I almost cried. Why couldn't my mother be like that?

"What's the news?" Tommy said to me. "Why you carrying that bag?"

"Forget it," I told him. "Let's go."

We ran down to the ironworks. Along the shore, the waves barely lapped the rocks, and it seemed the entire harbor had settled down before the crossing of ferries and tugs would tear it all up again. We pulled the raft from behind a heap of metal and dragged it into the water. He tossed in his shoes, and I dropped my bundle on top of them.

"Let's go way out today," I said. I looked across the harbor toward Castle Island. Let's explore the fort."

He put his hand above his eyes and scanned the water. "Really? I don't think we can go that far."

"You're the one who's always saying we could take the raft all the way to Florida," I said. "It'll be an adventure, like going to the South Seas."

"What if we can't get that far?"

"Then we'll go in the channel."

"OK," he said. "That's not so bad." But for the first time, I thought he didn't want to go on the raft at all.

He was still afraid of the water. I mentioned the channel because the banks were close enough to seem safe if something happened. But any distance is too far if you can't swim.

Tommy pulled the flag out of his pocket, and I gave him ten fingers to tie it to the mast. Then he sat on the deck, and I stepped into the water to shove off.

"You left your shoes on, dummy," he said to me.

"That's 'cuz the rocks hurt my feet."

"You go home with wet shoes, your mother's gonna kill you."

"Let me worry about that," I told him. Like I cared about wet shoes today.

I remember the sun was really bright that morning, and the reflection on the water made it twice as bad. Once we were fifty yards out, I figured we were nothing more than a black splotch to anybody on shore. I climbed in and we paddled to the middle of the channel. It led to the Charlestown Navy Yard, where Old Ironsides was docked, and then on to the Charles River. The windows on buildings along the shore blazed red and orange in the morning sun.

After a while, we got tired and rested. The raft bobbed on the waves, starting to shake us up a little.

"Maybe we should go back," said Tommy.

"How come?"

"We've never been this far out before." We couldn't have been more than a hundred yards out, not even close to the middle of the harbor, but I couldn't have him whining now. Somehow I was getting to the other side of the water, whether he came or not.

"Yeah, but look over there — we're practically to the fort. We could pretend that we've been shipwrecked there. Maybe we'll find treasure."

"Maybe," he said doubtfully. Then he said, "No, let's go back."

"No," I said. I needed to get to the other side. Whether he came with me or not.

"I want to go home," Tommy said. "Kick us back to Noodle Island."

"Let's play pirates instead."

"Giorgio, I'm scared."

"Don't be." Funny thing is, I was trying to get myself to the same place I saw him when those dirty Irish wrecked our first boat. But Tommy was the one who had what I needed: that fire in the belly.

He looked at me in desperate anger. "If you don't start kicking, I'll call you Sticky."

"You know how much I hate that," I told him calmly. "If

I were you, I wouldn't do it." I was telling him the truth, but I knew he'd never listen to me.

"Sticky, Sticky, afraid to kicky!" Just to scare him a bit, I rocked the boat even more. He shut up, but then he started to yell at me.

"Take us home! You're just being mean, and I don't want to be your friend anymore. Sticky, Sticky, Sticky, he's afraid to kicky!"

I splashed him then, and then he rushed me. I wasn't expecting it, but I handled it as if it was what I'd planned all along.

I let him take one swing at me. That's all I could afford. When it came, I waited till the last second before I moved. It was easy to dodge on that bouncing raft, and when he missed me, he was way off balance. I grabbed his arm and without even thinking, flung him overboard.

He came up spluttering once, screaming at me. "Help me, Giorgio, help me! I'll be nice, I'll be your friend! Help me, I can't swim!"

He was awfully loud for someone trying to save his breath. That loud, someone was going to hear him, even though I couldn't see anyone on either shore.

I grabbed a paddle. If anybody was watching, they'd see me reaching out to save him. Then I thought of something my mother once said to me: *"In ancient times, they thought that when you killed an animal, you got its power."* I brought the blade across to the side of his head. Blood poured from his ear, and he started crying, from anger or fear, I couldn't tell. I heard him say, "I'll kill…" but then I pushed him under mid-scream. He didn't come back up.

My chest was heaving as I watched the shadow sinking. It didn't take long to disappear entirely in that black harbor. For a second I couldn't believe what I had done, but then I remembered what Papa had told me, about family being more important than friends. And right now, I knew I had to sacrifice one to avenge the other.

The boat was close to the North End shore, right by where the molasses tank had been. I figured the distance at about fifty yards. I was tired from rowing and fighting, but I knew I could make it, though I'd have to leave the bundle of clothes behind. I kicked out one of the sides of the boat and jumped into the cold water. I never liked being in the harbor. I always thought something was swimming right under me, waiting to strike. This time, I had a picture of Tommy, one hand reaching up for my ankle to drag me down. It made me kick faster than his stupid name-calling ever did.

When I reached shore, I climbed a rusty ladder set in the sea wall, and sat there until I dried off. I could see the raft in the middle of the channel, tossed about by the waves, the little red flag just a silhouette. Eventually it drifted to the middle of the harbor, and the last I saw, it capsized in the wake of a tug.

Later on, I met a shoeshine boy. I had to give him a bloody nose before he'd hand over some of his black shoe polish. I combed it through my hair to hide the patch of white I inherited from my father. Then I began my life as George Jameson. I was already planning my revenge.

Chapter 7

Summer 1967

Mr. Nameless is doing his best impression of me slumped in the Delta, my gun in his hand, but I'm having a time wiping his blood out of the Cadillac. I got his coat ripped up into rags, but after cleaning off most of the seat and windshield, they're soaked through, and all they're doing now is pushing gobs of brains and bone into nasty little piles. I pull off my shoes and strip off my socks to finish off the steering wheel and dashboard. They're not much better, but it'll have to do.

Shoes back on my bare feet, I ease the Caddy up to the end of the warehouse and open the trunk. Suddenly a new plan springs to mind. The guy came prepared, with a jerry can of gas. I grab it and fish a book of matches out of my pocket, then walk back to the Olds.

The gas washes away the blood from his half a face. I splash more across the front and back seats. The scene is ugly, but it needs to be done. I'm feeling light headed, but that's just the fumes and the blood. The pounding in my head, that's the sound of the waves, right? What else could it be?

I toss the jerry can into the car and step back. I light one of the matches then shove it back into the book. It catches and I throw the little ball of flame into the Olds. It makes a short, bright arc, and then I hear and feel the *whoomp* of the gas catching. In a second, the interior is engulfed with flames, and Mr. Nameless is a dark spot in the middle of flickering orange and thick smoke. He seems to move, like a ghost, but I don't stick around to see it. I've got other things to do. I make my way back to the Eldorado, my shadow dancing in front of me.

As I go to shut the trunk, I hear a shoe scrape against the ground. It's not mine, and it's not from the direction of the burning car.

I can feel the heat of the car fire on my back. It comes in waves that wrap around me, heavy and suffocating, and it sounds like the breathing of a huge and scaly dragon.

But it's that scraping shoe that stops me with my hands against the lid of the trunk.

"You thought he was alone?" a voice says. "You're not too smart, are you?"

"Smart enough," I say. "I did what needed to be done."

"What was that?"

But I don't get to answer. The fire reaches the gas tank, and the explosion lifts the Olds. It lights up the night and knocks us both over. I feel the shudder of the car hitting the ground before I hear it, and pellets of molten glass singe my neck and back.

I'm up before the other guy, but just barely. He's on his knees, scrambling for his gun. I kick him in the chin, and I hear his teeth snap shut with a *clack*. I grab him by the collar and rap him against the ground. "How'd you find me so fast?" I say, knocking him again.

When he opens his mouth, blood spills down his chin. I think I took off part of his tongue with that kick. "How'd you do it?" I say.

"We've been on you since you got into that car." He sounds drunk. "You think the boss didn't have men around the neighborhood? You wouldn't have made it out of the house if it weren't for the fact that his bodyguard was taking a crap."

I hadn't realized I'd come that close to getting whacked myself, but it proves that Fate is watching over me. I did the right thing. The rest is clean up, that's all.

"How many are there?" I say. "Where are they?" I look up and try to see beyond the circle of light, but I can't see anyone else. Not yet.

He shakes his head, and gobs of blood fly off his lips. It looks black in the dying flickers of the car fire. I can hear sirens, and they're not too far away. Suddenly, he's fighting back, scrabbling his hands at my face, twisting his way out of my grip. I drop him and stand up, trying to step back, but he's got my ankle, and pulls me down. The thud shoots up my spine, and in that second, he's straddling me.

"You killed two good people tonight," he says. "And you're gonna pay for it." He gets in one nasty slug to my face before I push him off. Then we're both on our feet. I've got my hands on his neck, and he's pummeling my gut. The sirens are closer. I turn him around, like we're dancing, and get him up against the Cadillac. His face is turning dark, but he's not giving up the fight. I squeeze tighter and slam him against the car. He loses his footing, and that's what I need. With one more thrust, I crack his head on the lid of the trunk, and stun him enough to shove him in and close it.

The guy is banging and screaming in the trunk. I can get rid of him later, but right now I've got to take care of myself. "Two good people," he said. Bullshit. I start the car and drive it past the Olds. The fire's almost out now, and the shadows are creeping in from the water again. I get back on the access road and pass the fire trucks and a police car. Before the cops have a chance to turn around, I'm on the highway heading south. His screaming is louder, and I hear the fear in his voice.

It crowds out the other screams in my head.

Exhibit for the Defense

"I never betrayed a soul," she says to me.

"You slut, you forced Papa out of the house, then you took up with him. You knew exactly what you were doing. The two of you had my father killed."

"That's a lie," she says.

"Not a word of it."

She's wringing her hands. "It's all a lie," she insists. "When they found your raft, I ran all the way to the water. They found Tommy's body, but never yours. I lost your father and you both in the same week."

"You mean you screwed us both over in the same week."

"What good would that have done?"

"You saw Papa was in trouble, and you just stayed at home fucking his best friend."

"Whatever I did, I did for you and your father."

"You're a goddamned whore. And I'm going to kill you for it."

She stands up straight. "How dare you presume to know what I did? When you were gone, I had nothing. All my life, I scrimped and saved. I got nothing from your father. But I stood by him to the end. When I thought you were dead, I did everything I was supposed to. I waked you both in my house. I put wreaths on the door and stopped the clocks at the hours you each died for a whole year. Peter was there to help me, and where were you?"

Chapter 8
Summer 1967

The Cadillac eats up the road like a hungry beast. Whoever that guy I wasted was, he knew how to buy a car, that's for sure. He got all the options — bucket seats with headrests, cruise control, automatic climate control. He even went for the AM/FM stereo. I turn it on, and hit the buttons looking for anything that'll make noise. Between the sound of the front tires and the banging in the trunk, I need something to calm my nerves.

The heat of the road sneaks in even though I've got the climate control blowing full force. I'm dripping with sweat, and it's hard to catch my breath. Cars come and go, some stay behind a while, then get replaced by others. I have no idea if any of them are after me. Maybe my passenger was blowing smoke up my ass when he said there were others, maybe he wasn't. But this pounding in my head, it's gotta stop. I'd like to hit a bar along the way, just knock back one or two shots. It might do me a lot of good, but I can't risk it. Either someone'd hear him, or else someone might recognize me. Sweet Jesus, though, I'd like a drink. Or even some of that stuff Liz smokes — *smoked*. Anything to steady my nerves, to make it quiet. Christ, Liz. I can't even think about her now. There's been too much blood.

The radio is playing some of that hippie shit. The announcer said it's called "A Day in the Life," but all I hear is noise. That's been my day, a lot of noise. Is that an alarm clock? Time to get off this highway, hit the back roads. I get off at the Kent exit, heading west. There's a good amount of woods around here. I'll get rid of the guy in the trunk, then head into Connecticut. Maybe New York City's too hot for me. I'll just head into upstate New York, see what happens.

Everything's dark. What few houses I pass, the lights are out and everyone's asleep. No one dreams about what's driving past their safe little lives, what's about to happen. The road narrows, and the trees get thicker. Fireflies drift around the car and scatter as I push deeper into the forest. Branches cover the road like a tunnel, and I can't see the sky. The Eldorado's headlights are like a pair of searchlights waving across the winding road. They pick out a dirt road up ahead, and I follow them where they lead, slowing down to leave as little of a trail as I can. I hit some ruts, and the guy in the trunk screams. He knows what's happening. He'll probably know the place we end up.

I see eyes lighting up in the bushes as we pass. Deer, I guess. Maybe raccoons. They'll be the only witnesses.

When the Caddy won't go forward anymore, I stop. The guy goes quiet. He's making a plan. I hear him scuffling around. What would I do? Get on my back, be ready to kick when the hood went up. Or maybe crouch on all fours, spring up like a frog. Fine.

I turn off the engine and get out, leaving the door open, and I walk around to the back. Holding the .38 in one hand, I put the key in the lock with the other. I can't hear him. He's holding his breath, ready to act. I'm in a hurry, but I've got a few minutes. So I wait, standing on one side, reaching over. When I think I've got him good and rattled, I turn the key. He jumps, pushing the hood up, leaping out in front of me, and there I am with the gun aimed and ready. "Sit down," I say.

He looks at me, and in the dark, the wound on his head is a black streak. His eyes are as used to the dark as mine, of course, so this is the only advantage I have. "Sit down," I tell him again, and he does.

For the first time I get a good look at him. Dark pants, turtleneck sweater. Nice shoes. Tassels. He's done all right for himself.

"How'd you make me so fast?" I ask.

"I ain't telling you anything," he says. "You're a dead man, whether you kill me or not."

"You got that right," I say. "Now tell me what I don't know."

"Fuck you." I bring the butt of the gun down on his head, and he winces and shakes.

"All right," I say, grabbing the back of his neck. "We're going for a walk in the woods, but we ain't coming back together, right?"

He strains against me, but I've got the muzzle in his side. We march until I can just barely see the roof light on the Cadillac. We're not that deep at all, but what can I do? It'll be enough.

"Last chance to come clean," I say. "Who's on to me?"

"We got guys from all over," he laughs. "You hit the boss, you dumb shit. They'll be on you until you croak, one way or another. They called Providence, New Haven, New York, even up north, in New Hampshire and Maine. You're as hot as they come."

"But it was personal for you, wasn't it?" I say. "What did he do for you?"

"He brought me up," he says. "His wife, too. Like I was their kid. Sunday dinners and everything."

"She ever tell you she had a kid?" I say.

"Yeah, he died."

"Then you and me got a couple of things in common," I say. The woods light up for a second as the bullet passes

through his head. I hear something jump and run in the
bushes, then it's quiet again. I walk back to the car, my head
still pounding. Maybe I can get that drink now.

So she did remember me, even before I showed up.

Chapter 9

Summer 1929

After I climbed out of the harbor, I got rid of my old life the way a snake sheds its skin. I rubbed shoe polish in my hair to cover the streak of white. The last thing I needed was for some shnook to recognize me. I lived on the street for about a week, sleeping in alleys, stealing fruit. I couldn't help wondering if I was ripping off Sweet 'n' Fine fruit carts, but I didn't care so long as I had something in my belly. During the day, I wandered through town, trying to stay busy. Mostly I stuck around Scollay Square. Nobody bothered you in the Square. It's funny, how safe it was, when Tommy was so afraid to go in. To earn a few pennies, I ran errands for guys, picking up newspapers and stuff.

Towards the end of the week, the shoe polish in my hair started to wear off. I found another shoeshine kid. I was too tired and hungry to take him. I offered him a few cents to let me rub some polish in my hair.

"Whacha wanna do that for?" he asked. "You on the lam?"

"Yeah, what of it?"

"Nothin," he said, wide-eyed. "Wish I was on the lam."

"So, you gonna let me have it or not?"

"Sure, and it won't cost ya nothin." I rubbed my fingers in the can and ran them through my hair. "Where you been sleepin'?" he said.

"Wherever I can," I told him while I was combing the thick stuff through my hair, fighting the knots and dirt.

"Tell you what," he said. "Ma wouldn't mind if you stayed with us. If you did some work, you could pay for your food. I swear, I won't tell her or no one you're on the run. It'd be swell. What's your name?"

"George," I said. It felt strange coming out of my mouth, but I knew I could get used to it.

"I'm Stu Kowalski. Call me Stooky. Come on, I'll bring you home."

He threw his polish and rags in a wooden box and led me to his house in the West End, on the other side of Scollay Square. Both are gone now, replaced by a huge brick waste-land around that ugly new City Hall, but at one time, they were the heart of the city.

He led me down to Green Street, to the corner of Staniford. Stooky was a small kid, and he kind of rolled when he walked. He seemed to know everyone, and they all looked me over like I'd just climbed out of the grave. The neighborhood was crowded and smelled of rotting garbage. The tenements looked like they were about to fall into each other. Laundry hung out to dry across the streets, and people had to yell to be heard above everybody else. It made East Boston look like wide open fields. It was the most comfortable feeling I've ever had.

Stooky ran up the three floors to his apartment, and I was out of breath by the time I caught up to him. The hallway reeked of cabbage. There was only a hint of garlic. I wondered if anyone around here was Italian.

I finally made it up the stairs as he burst into his apart-ment, calling out, "Ma! Ma! Come quick!"

A woman with the face and arms of a dock worker, wear-ing an apron and holding a steaming pot, looked in from the kitchen. "What'sa matter?" she asked, without sounding too concerned.

"This is my friend George," he said, pulling me through the front room. "He's got no place to sleep, so I told him he could stay with us."

"What?" she yelled. Then she started ranting in some language I'd never heard. I found out later it was Polish. The yelling echoed off the bare, dingy walls, and she was pointing at me and random things in the kitchen by turns. Stooky yelled back just as loud. I no idea where it was all leading, but she finally turned to me and said, "You really sleep a week in street?"

I nodded, playing the sad little kid as best I could.

"What happened?" she asked.

I looked at the floor. "My ma died, no one was left to take me in. The police were trying to put me in a home, so I ran off."

"Ach, police! What about you father?"

"Don't know. He's never around."

She nodded. You heard that story every day. "You stay here, you live my rules. Rule number one: you pay. I don't got enough money to feed us, never mind a stranger off the street. You gotta get a job."

"I will," I said solemnly.

"And you go to school. I find you skip, I send you right outta here. No hellion what's gambling and skipping school sleep in my house."

"No, ma'am," I said.

She said something else to Stooky in Polish. He turned to me and said, "Ma says you can stay, but you gotta take a bath. She says you smell like cabbage that's been boiled too long." Mrs. Kowalski laughed and went back into the kitchen. Stooky took me to the bath house where I scrubbed cold water on me with a stiff brush, and an hour later, red raw but clean, I sat down to my first meal with my new family.

Besides Stooky and his mother, there was also Mr. Kowalski, who spoke no English. The whole time I was there, I never saw him out of bed. Mrs. Kowalski brought him soup, and I heard him slurping it in the next room. Stooky said it was some accident he had at work.

And then there was Rose. She was almost thirteen, and already looked much older, with long light brown hair and the makings of an impressive bosom. She wanted to be as American as possible, which caused no end of fighting between her and her mother. The only time it was quiet was when Rose was either helping her father eat, or when she was out. She said she was doing errands, but more than once I saw her at a lunch counter having a tonic with one pale American boy or another.

The day after Stooky brought me home, Rose enrolled me at the Mayhew School around the corner. She told the Principal I was her cousin just come from the Midwest to stay with her. She gave me a lunch pail and told me to come home right after school, because my "aunt" needed me to help around the apartment. Then Rose was gone, and the secretary led me to a classroom across the hall from Stooky's. He was in the fourth grade, and they put me in the third. No one noticed I was Italian and not Polish. To the American teachers, there wasn't a difference anyway.

I got a job selling newspapers before and after school, and gave the money to Mrs. Kowalski. She put it in a jar on the top shelf in the kitchen. I slept on old blankets on the parlor floor next to Stooky. When it got cold, we shared the mat to keep warm.

For the most part, I lived by the rules Mrs. Kowalski gave me. I gave her most of the money I made, about fifty cents a week, and I almost never skipped school, especially in the winter. I went home with Stooky after all my papers were sold, and his mother always made us something sweet to eat before we did our chores.

Saturdays, Stooky and me, and sometimes Rose, went

to the movie house to see a picture. Usually we went to the Lancaster on Causeway Street. We loved the cowboy and adventure serials. Rose liked the romantic movies, but us boys couldn't stand them. We just waited for the hero to slug someone. I liked living with my new family.

I'd been living with the Kowalski's about two years when I got a better job, cleaning up at another movie theater nearby, the RKO Keith, over on Washington Street. It paid a dollar a week, and I saw all the movies I wanted for free. It was a great job. Sometimes I forgot where I was until the picture finished and the hall lit up again. I worked hard, because this was one job I didn't want to lose. I kept hoping that one day, I'd be promoted from custodian to running the projector.

I'd just turned twelve. I remember because we ran *Little Caesar* with Edward G. Robinson for an extra two weeks. After that, some time in February, we got a new movie, *Cimarron*, starring Richard Dix as Yancey Cravat. It was a huge movie, twelve reels. I remember sitting there, watching Dix be everything — pioneer, owner of a newspaper owner, statesman, millionaire. But the best part was when he was getting ready to grab land in the Territory. Until then, the movie had been shown on the regular sized screen. Then, when all the wagons were lined up, the curtains pulled back, showing the full length of the screen. Horses and carriages stretched out forever, it seemed. I watched that movie about twenty times, and every single time that curtain pulled back, I was excited as the first time.

Cimarron showed me I could be whatever I wanted. Yancey became my hero, someone who didn't care what others thought. Like when he wrote that editorial about how great the Indians were. No one liked it, but after a while, everyone thought it was the best thing he had ever done, and every year they published it again in his paper. He could go off for years at a time, whenever he wanted, and when he came back, there was his wife, waiting for him. That's exactly what I want, I decided.

Pretty soon I was hanging out with other kids in the neighborhood, learning new ways to make extra money. Sometimes Stooky ran with us, but for the most part, he wasn't interested. They called themselves "The Gang," like they were the only one around. The kid that brought me in was Max Diamond. He was sort of the leader, but we all took the lead one time or another. We did little shit, B & E's and petty shoplifting. Sometimes we snuck into the burlesque houses in Scollay Square and watched the dancing girls do their strip teases. We did protection for the younger kids in the neighborhood. It wasn't until I got my next legit job that we pulled real capers.

By then I was fifteen, still living with Stooky and his family. I was running the projector by now, but it didn't pay enough anymore. My boss sent me to a friend of his who ran a bunch of theaters around town. This guy was looking for someone who could do anything: clean, paint, hang posters — no problem — and to drive the car, which could've been a problem. But I told him I drove like the best chauffeurs in Europe, and he believed me. The next thing I knew, I was driving a loop around town.

See, the owner of these theaters was a cheapskate. When a new movie came to town, he only ordered one set of reels for his whole operation. He staggered the start times, and it was my job was to start a movie at one place, then to take the used reels to the next one, then to the next, all the way around. All day, I drove in a circle, picking up and dropping off reels. That's how I showed one copy of a movie at four different movie houses, all at the same time.

Within a few weeks, I really did become an expert driver. I learned how to "whip" corners, which meant taking them so fast the car went up on two wheels. Every time I got pulled over by the police, all I had to do was show them a card that said to send any citations to my boss. Pretty soon, they didn't even bother stopping me, and I didn't even have a license!

That card was our ticket to the big time. Whenever one of the other kids from the Gang pulled a job, he did it when he knew I'd be coming by on my way to deliver the next reel. All he had to do was jump on the running board for a few blocks, jump off, and be a mile away from the scene. A perfect set-up. After a while, I had someone or other on my running boards for most of the trip. Only once did someone fall off, while I was whipping the car and forgot to tell him. He broke his arm on the cobblestones, but no one ever caught him.

By now I was making pretty good money, and getting sick of handing it over to Mrs. Kowalski. I don't know what happened to her, but it seemed that the more money I gave her the more suspicious and upset she got. She'd get angry when I gave her a few dollars. Then, one time, Rose came home with her latest American boyfriend, some law clerk with swanky clothes and not much personality. We were sitting in the parlor, and I caught him gawking at Rose's enormous chest. I didn't blame him, because I did the same whenever I could, too. I said to him, "Watch it, buddy,"

I was watching out for the family, but Mrs. Kowalski just heard me mouthing off to a "lawyer," the guy she thought was going to make her daughter rich. She just started in on me, asking why I couldn't be a nice boy like this one, her soon-to-be son-in-law. The guy gulped when she said that, and Rose shot him a warning look. Don't butt in, it said. At least her mother wasn't picking on her this time, calling her a tramp or worse.

"Why you never come in regular time? What you do in the street?" the woman said to me.

"Better things than what happens here," I told her.

That was the first time in almost six years that Mr. Kowalski acknowledged me. He was sitting with us in the parlor, wrapped up in a heap of blankets. He didn't understand what I said, but he knew what I meant. He hauled off and hit me on the side of the head, knocking me to the floor. Who knew he had that kind of strength in him? Rose screamed and her boyfriend looked lost, wondering what he was getting himself into. Stooky looked down on me and said, "Don't ever talk to my mother that way again."

It was time to leave. After everything I had done, the whole family, except maybe Rose, had turned against me. I brought in more money than anybody else, even when I held some back, and they had no gratitude whatsoever. I grabbed my things — a few changes of clothes and a couple of pairs of leather shoes — threw them in a sack, and was out of the house in two minutes flat. No one even said good-bye.

Chapter 10
Summer 1967

This car reeks. I thought I left Mr. Nameless behind, but his blood is everywhere. My hands are sticking to the wheel. There's nothing for it, I've got to boost another car. Problem is, it's too hot to leave it where they'll find it. On the other hand, who'd expect me to cut through the woods of Rhode Island? So I have to push on. When I get across Connecticut, then I'll be able to ditch it. I should torch it, too, but that'll just call attention. No, better to leave it in the corner of a parking lot, sometime in the morning. If I make it that far.

Meanwhile, the ruts on this goddamned dirt road'll kill the shocks. Then what will I do? Walk? That'd make me the last in this parade of dead bodies. How many has it been? Two hoods, that pussy Bricks, and *her*. And then there's Liz and… But that wasn't my fault. It was fate. Maybe she got too close to me, maybe I encouraged it. But she knew what she was doing. Knew who I am. She knew a hundred doctors, and she could've had it taken care of if she wanted. She knew the score.

I mean, it's not like we met at a Sunday School picnic. But some girls think they can change the world. That's one thing my mother could have told her, with one of her goddamned Greek fairy tales. You don't get in front of fate.

The trees crowd against the road. I've left the state park,

but you wouldn't know it except for a small house here and there. The road twists like a snake, and even with the headlights, I could easily crash into this wall of trees. Sometimes, that doesn't seem like a bad idea. The headlights still set eyes blazing in the darkness, and I wonder what is it beyond the safety of the road, waiting to get me?

That's it, I'm talking crazy to myself. I need that drink. There's too much pounding in my head. The next tavern or cocktail lounge I find, I'm stopping. It's still early, after all that's happened tonight, not even eleven o'clock. There's got to be some place open in this town that serves a shot and a beer. I'm getting dizzy turning this wheel.

There. Looks like a roadhouse. A few bikes parked in the dirt lot, but the way I'm feeling tonight, bikers could get more trouble than they could give. I've got nothing to lose anymore.

I park on the side, out of the light. When I get out, I wipe my clothes off best I can. I still look a mess. There's dirt on my knees and arms, and I'm sure that stinging over my eye means there's good-sized cut. Probably getting a shiner, too. I tuck the .38 in the back of my pants, cover it with my shirttails, and go inside.

A screeching guitar and incoherent lyrics shoot out of the dark. The clink of a cue ball somehow carries over that, and I sit at the bar. The late news is on, but the sound is off. Same shit, anyhow. Helicopters and guns, grunts humping through the jungle. What a fucking mess. None of our goddamned business, but we're in it now.

"You look like shit," the bartender says, and I look past him at the dusty mirror.

My face floats above the bottlenecks, and I see he's right. The cut over my eye stretches to my cheek, and, for good or for bad, something — soot? blood? — blacks out the streak of white in my hair. I got smudges of dirt and soot on my clothes, but it's probably too dark to see any blood that isn't mine.

"Keep your opinions to yourself," I say. "I want a shot of bourbon, and a bottle of something cold."

He turns, muttering something that sounds like "asshole," but he gets me a Narragansett, and I hold the bottle to my forehead and eyes before I drink. I hadn't realized my throat was so dry until it refuses the first gulp. I force it down, then smooth it with another swallow. When I put the bottle down, I see the shot, brown and inviting, in front of me. I knock it back, then sip at the 'Gansett. That bloody face is staring at me, so I wave at the bartender, point to the shot glass, and make my way to the bathroom.

Along the way, I pass the guys playing pool, and a couple of girls out for the night. In a couple of booths, a few other hicks, but no one special. I push open the door to the toilet and find myself in a room the size of a phone booth, with a crapper and a sink and a bulb hanging off a cord. Someone scratched, "suck my snake" on the mirror. It shows up double across my eyes.

A thin trickle of cold water is all I get when I turn the handles, and the soot turns to mud before I can start rubbing and scraping it off. Three days of stubble rasp against my hand. It seems like I'm there ten minutes trying to splash the drips up to my face, but soon enough I look OK. Even the cut doesn't look half bad. I head back out to my drink.

I can't have been gone that long — the news is still on. The Sox dropped a double header to the Senators. Those bastards won't amount to anything this year. I shake my head at the futility of it all, and I notice one of the girls is gone, but the other is sitting next to my beer. She's got her back to me, and I take a second to get the picture.

She's got dark hair down to her shoulders, and a white blouse, short-sleeved and tight, tucked into Capri pants. One foot is hooked behind the other, and I can see painted nails sticking out of her open-toed high heels. She's leaning with one elbow on the bar, and her other hand is spinning a half-empty shot glass. Nice.

I sit down, and we look at each other. She's older than I expected, but still good-looking. Maybe she's got only twenty years of bad road compared to my thirty. The dim lighting hides the lines I know are there, but her eyes are sharp and slitted, like a cat's.

"What happened to you?" she says with a smile, like it's all a big joke. Her husky voice cuts through the fog in my mind.

"Honey, you wouldn't believe me in a million years. You gonna finish that?"

She glances at her glass, then pushes it towards me. "Looks like you need it more than me," she says, and I knock it back.

One last news story about the war. They're showing long-haired kids with bandanas and signs. I nod at the screen. "You don't see much of that around here, do you?"

Instead of answering, she waves the peace sign, then drops her index finger. "Thatta girl," I say. "Let's have another."

"What's your name?" she asks.

"Jim." The way she smiles you can tell she doesn't believe me, and doesn't care.

"I'm Alice," she says. Okay, if that's what she wants me to believe.

Another couple more and we're like old friends. I notice they have a story of the burnt-out car near the end of the news, but no one's watching. She slides her hand across the bar and puts it over mine. "Let's go," she says.

But before I can say anything, the door bangs open. I turn around to see what the commotion is and catch a glimpse of a couple of toughs, or, when I see more clearly, kids trying to be toughs. They slide in like they want trouble, their slicked-back hair reflecting the light of red and blue neon like the skin of a reptile. "Let's go," Alice says again, more urgently.

"You know them?" I say.

"Everyone does. The local mafia." She looks away, trying to be inconspicuous.

"Those creeps? They should be ordering milkshakes. Finish your drink, darling. We got all night." But even as I say it, I know it's a lie. I doubt they're mobbed up, but that doesn't mean they're not dangerous. Just the opposite.

One of them slides into the chair next to me. He bobs his head and smiles, like we're friends. I roll my eyes away from him, back to Alice.

"Rough night?" the kid says, but I ignore him. It's the first step in this dance, and even though I know how it ends, I gotta follow the music.

The other one, I see in the mirror, sits behind me, at the same table where Alice and her friend had been when I first walked in. He slouches, with his legs open, one hand dangling near his crotch. Classy.

"Let's have a drink," the first one says.

"I've already got one, junior," I say. "Isn't this a school night?"

"Nope, school's out for the summer. Why don't you buy me a shot to celebrate, huh? I'll have whatever you're having."

I look him full in the face. "Son, I'm having a hell of a night. Trust me, you don't want any part of it."

The other one sidles up next to Alice, and she tries to shrink against me. Not much comfort there, she realizes, but she already made her decision.

"You giving my friend a hard time?" he says to me, talking over Alice's head. "We're just trying to be friendly, why you being rude?"

Just then the bartender puts a pair of bottles on the counter, then fishes out another one for me. He's got a worried look on his face. He's seen this dance before, too.

"Thanks, Sully," says the first one, and his partner raises his own bottle in a salute. I leave mine where it is, with a drop of water oozing down the label.

"Listen," I say. "I'm having a private talk with my lady friend here. Take a walk, why don't you?"

"I thought I'd like a ride. That your Cadillac outside?"

"You want it? Take it. I'll get another."

They laugh. I'm serious, but they're too dumb to realize. The first one takes out a switchblade, and even over the loud rock 'n' roll, I can hear the hiss of it flicking open.

I knew a kid like this when I was inside at Walpole. I can still remember him with that same nervous energy, pacing the cell, waiting for the warden to come and tell him it was all a big mistake. He was innocent, he kept saying. It wasn't his fault, he was gonna get made, he had never done anything wrong in his life. Rambling whatever shit he thought sounded hard. We were together in that cell a long time, and I know he wasn't that tough at lights out. The only thing he had going for him was that he actually had done something bad enough to put him in maximum security. These punks didn't rate a night in the local pokey.

"Put that away," I say quietly. "Put it away and go home." I put my hand over the .38 sitting on the small of my back, and he gets the message. He nods at his friend, and they get up to leave. Alice slumps on the bar, suddenly deflated. The worst is over, and I won. I smile at her, and I'm ready to take her up on her offer to go.

I'm already bending backwards before the pain registers. The punch to the kidneys knocks me off the stool, and Alice spills her drink as I crack my head on the floor.

The whole place is scuffling and shouting as I try to stand up. I reach for the rung on the stool, but I grab Alice's ankle instead and she screams. A boot slams into my belly, and another to the side of my head. I hear glass breaking and tables falling over, but I can't focus my eyes, except to see there's a chip in the red paint on one of Alice's toes. She screams again, and it pierces my eyeballs. The toenails are gone, replaced by one of the black boots that keep me down here. I see hands scrabbling at my neck, and feel another going for the .38.

I reach back quick enough to grab it and swing it out. My arm keeps flying until the barrel connects with the first guy's ear. There's a double *thunk* as his head bounces between the gun and the counter, and it gives me enough time to stand up.

The gun clears the area around me the way light scatters cockroaches. Even the bikers, holding cue sticks like clubs, step back. I see Alice is in the arms of the second kid, his switchblade poking through her white blouse. The look on his face shows even more fear than hers does, and it tells me it won't take much for him to push the blade in. The first kid has recovered from the bump on the bar, and he's standing between us, his arms stretched out like he's trying to introduce us. His head flicks back and forth, trying to take it all in.

I lower the gun, enough to look reasonable. "Let her go," I say. "Don't be stupid." But he holds the knife tighter against her, and she squirms under its pressure.

"Don't shoot, don't shoot," he's yelling. He's too scared to listen to me, just sane enough to realize I could shoot him before he could stab her. "Don't shoot," he keeps saying, and it's like there's never been another sound in the world, he's so loud.

The other one says, "Let's get out of here." He looks at me and says, "Gimme the keys, we're taking your car and you can have her."

"You don't want that car," I say. Alice looks like I just stabbed her myself.

"Gimme the keys!" He reaches over to me, as if the gun doesn't exist.

My eyes still on the knife, I reach into my jacket pocket and toss them over. He catches them and crosses between us, giving his friend enough cover to break for the door. Before Sully can bring Alice a soothing shot, we all hear the Caddy spitting gravel and peeling out of the lot.

I know we haven't got much time before the punks calm down and notice what's all over the seat and dashboard, so I let Alice have her shot and then hustle her to her feet. "Let's go." She nods and slips her arm around my waist. One of the bikers says, "Hey, man, we can catch him," but I wave him off and we slip out the door.

"Which is your car? Where are the keys?" I fumble through her purse, and that wakes her up. She plucks them out of the mess of cigarettes, coins, and whatever else she keeps in there and points to a blue Ford. I get her in, slide next to her, and turn the key.

Nothing.

I turn it again, still nothing. "Sometimes it does that," she says from far away. "Try again."

This time, it rumbles to life and I reverse without looking. When we get on the road, I say, "Where's your place?" She points vaguely down the road and I follow the direction.

After a mile or so, Alice comes to herself. "You son of a bitch!" she screams, punching me backhanded on the shoulder, hard enough to make me swerve. "You were gonna let him kill me! Look!" She scrabbles at her blouse, and I look down. By the light of the dash I see a dark spot against the white of her skin. "He stabbed me, and all you cared about was your goddamned car!"

"He was never going to do more than that," I say. "Shut up and let me drive. Where the hell am I going?"

"Turn there," she says too late, and I have to skid my way onto an unlit road. "There," she says after we pass a few widely spaced houses. "That's my place."

It's a bungalow no bigger than my first apartment in the West End. There's a propane tank attached to the outside wall in the driveway, and the yard is nothing but a carpet of pine needles.

I cut the engine and climb out to help her stand up, but she leads the way to the door. It's unlocked and she holds my hand as she leads me into the dark kitchen. The door's not closed before she turns on me, kissing me hard, reaching for my belt. Her tongue slides over my teeth, reaching deeper, then pulls out and finds my ear, my neck, and she's biting, her hands frantic to get to my cock, and I'm not shy either. I push her past the table, turning her against the wall. She puts her hands up, feet back, like I'm a cop searching her, but she's looking back at me, begging for me, panting like a dog. I yank down her pants, ripping her panties at the same time, until there's just enough room to get in.

She screeches and her back arches, and she's leaning on one arm. The other reaches back at my legs, scratching till I'm bleeding. I get my arms around her, pulling her bra off, then squeezing her tits in time to the shaking of the wall. As I get closer to coming, her screams get louder and shorter and faster until we're both lost in the sound. In the middle of it all, I can feel the blood from her knife wound dripping onto my hands.

When we're done, hoarse and covered in sweat and blood, she says, "Now it's my turn." She shrugs out of her torn blouse, slips off her shoes and pants. I do the same and she leads me into the bedroom.

Even in the dark I can see that the room is nearly bare. There's nothing more than a full-sized bed, a bureau, and a vanity with a mirror. Our reflections are black ghosts flitting in the dark against the slightly lighter shadow of the doorway.

"Lie down," she says gently, and I do, without turning down the sheets. But instead of joining me, she goes back to the kitchen. I thought she'd want a slow throw, maybe straddle me then we'd fall asleep like babies. But now I hear clanging pans and running water.

"Yeah," I say, "I could eat like there's no tomorrow." It isn't until I say it that I realize there might not be a tomorrow. I might have had my last fuck, here in the woods with a girl whose real name I don't even know. I've lost anything I ever thought would make me happy, but instead of making me sad, this bare dark room reminds of my first time. That was in the dark, too. But by then I'd known Rose a long time.

Chapter 11

Summer 1967

"I'm not cooking at this time of night," Alice says, still making noise in the kitchen. A minute later she comes in carrying a metal tray. She puts it on the nightstand and turns on the small lamp. In the orange glow I see a bottle of iodine and a pan of steaming water. A couple of cloths are rolled up between the bottle and pan.

This is the first time I've seen her, really seen her, in good light. I was right, she's closer to my age than she was trying to look, but without her clothes on, without an act, I can tell she's seen a few things in her time. She's smiling, but there's little joy in it. The cut from the knife has stopped bleeding, but there are other, older marks on her arms and one on her side. It's raised and runs about four inches straight down to her hip. I reach out to follow it with my finger, but she flinches and I pull my hand back. I get the idea that she might have had her last fuck, too, here in the woods with a man whose real name she doesn't even know.

"We're a couple of tough old birds, aren't we?" I say to her, and for a second her smile is real.

"What happened tonight, before I met you?" she asks, dipping a cloth in the water. She wrings it out, and wipes the cut on my face. It smarts, but I know the iodine will be worse.

"I'm a long ways from home, that's for sure."

"I thought I was going to die tonight. Lucky you were there."

"If I hadn't, you wouldn't've been in that situation."

She dabs at my jaw and when she dips the cloth back in the pan, I see the water turn a nasty pink. Most of it isn't even my blood. "Still, I think it was fate you showed up."

"The funny thing about fate is," I tell her, "you never know what it's got in mind 'til it strikes."

"So what's your real name?"

"You first."

She shrugs, and it tightens up her tits. For a second I can tell what she looked like maybe twenty years ago. If I had known her then, I might never have come to this point.

"I told you," she said. "My name *is* Alice. But after teaching your kind for over twenty years, I can spot a lie before it leaves your lips. Who are you, really?"

I'm not ready to face that kind of question. "You're a teacher?" I say.

"Junior high History." She's using the second cloth now, drenching it in iodine.

"I never knew a teacher did stuff like that before." She laughs and brushes a hard nipple against my cheek, but I pull away. It reminds me of the last breast I saw, just a couple of hours ago, with a bullet hole in it. I can hear *her* voice starting up again. "*I gave you whatever strength you had,*" she's saying. "*Your father abandoned you long before he died.*" I reach out for the iodine and rub it into the cut on my head. It shuts that voice up quick.

"So talk," she says. Alice, I mean.

"I'm an orphan," I tell her. "I grew up on the streets." Which is strictly true. I don't tell her about Tommy, that doesn't matter. "When I lost my parents," I say, "I had to fend for myself. I pulled a little breaking and entering job and almost got caught, so I took off." I leave out my planning revenge, that it was my own mother's idea, from all those Greek fairy tales she told me. The one thing I learned from those stories was that you always avenge your father's murder. She dug her own grave. Otherwise I'm straight with Alice, mostly.

Chapter 12

Summer 1935

Six years after climbing out of Boston Harbor, I was fifteen and on my own. At first, I had fallen in with this kid Stooky Kowalski and his family, but now I had enough dough to get myself a small room on Green Street in the West End, not far from the apartment where I'd stayed with the Kowalskis. At this point, I'd already fallen out with Stooky and his mother, but I didn't need their help anymore. Between the legitimate work I did at the movie houses, which gave me access to the Depression glass I could sell on the side, and the jobs with the Gang, I was taking home over thirty dollars a week, more than some whole families.

I had other things going for me, too. I've always been good at picking up girls. One night, I was at the Old Howard, the burlesque house, and I swore that was Rose, Stooky's older sister, dancing in a line of bare-legged girls. She wore nothing but some flimsy pink underwear and a sparkly brassiere that strained to hold in her huge chest. I hadn't seen her in almost a year, since her mother kicked me out of the house just for making more money than anyone else in the family. I thought I'd catch up with an old friend, so I met her in the dim hallway outside the dressing room. Up close, the brassiere turned out to be nothing but spangles sewed onto something she could've bought at Raymond's, worn over a full-body covering. Even her legs were covered, it turned out. I didn't care.

"You dance great," I told her. "What's your name?"

"Camille," she said, not looking at me, just giving a guy the brush-off.

"Naw, your real name."

Then she looked at me. "George, is that you?"

I smiled and took her by the arm. "Well, *Camille*, you must be hungry after that show. Let's go over to Joe and Nemo's for a hot dog."

It was almost midnight, and as we walked up Cambridge Street, she asked if anybody would be looking for me.

"What are you talking about? I'm practically thirty! I've got my own place and everything!"

"Oh, yeah?" she said. "Prove it."

She wasn't too old herself, maybe about nineteen. She told me she'd left home not long after I did, hounded by her mother for being "that kind of girl."

She shrugged. "I decided I would be, if she thought that way." We were three blocks from her house, but she never went back. Never even saw my old friend Stooky, the one who'd taken me in while I was still dripping wet.

After getting the dogs, I walked her to my place. It wasn't that much, but it impressed her. "I still don't have my own apartment," she said. "I share a place with two other girls from the Howard." But not that night.

I showed Rose all my nice clothes, the suits I was buying. I had a bureau filled with shirts and silk socks. She ran her hands through them like she was searching for jewels in the sand. "They look like something a movie star would wear," she said. "Remember those movies we used to go to?"

The way she said it, I could tell she missed the old days. She was still a little girl in a lot of ways. We sat on the bed. "Shut the light," she said. "It'll be like when we were at the pictures." But then we both knew where it was going. It was my first time, but not hers, and even in the dark, just by the light of the streetlamps, she showed me what to do. I was a quick study.

While I went around with her, I was tops. All I had to do was bring her some flowers or candy, just cheap silly stuff, and I could do what I wanted with her. When we weren't in my bed, she got me into the dressing rooms, introduced me to a lot of people. One girl I met, Doris, did the make-up for the dancers and singers. She showed me how to color my hair, instead of using grease to cover up my white spot. It came in handy now that the Gang was pulling bigger, more sophisticated jobs.

Before I was seventeen, I had my own apartment, my pick of the best looking dancers in Scollay Square, and still hadn't been put in the clink. It couldn't get any better.

And then it got as bad as it could.

After about six months together, Rose started acting real cagey. Moody. Either I was the only one who ever loved her, or I was a shit. There was no middle ground with her. One day she wouldn't leave my place, even though she was headlining at the Old Howard that night. Just sat in my bed, crying about her ma.

"I miss her," she said. "I wanna go home."

"What the hell's keeping you?" I said. "She's three blocks away from here." It was getting late, and I had a meeting with Vic Spruce, one of my guys from the Gang. Shiny Max set us up, saying, "Georgie, you two will make a great team." I couldn't be late.

"She hates me," Rose said. "She'll call me a tramp."

"She did plenty of times before," I said. "What's the difference?"

Rose didn't answer, just cried harder. I looked at my watch. This couldn't go on much longer. I'd have to get her dressed and onto the stage myself.

"It's all her fault. I never would've been here if she hadn't turned so rotten. I hate my life, and it's all her fault."

"You hate being with me? What the hell are you doing naked in my bed, then?"

She ignored me, and that pissed me off. "I could've been a good girl, but she never trusted me. I could kill her for the way I ended up. That's what I'd do, wait for her and my useless father to go to sleep and kill 'em both."

"Would you really kill her?" I asked Rose.

She didn't answer my question. But I saw her thinking about it.

Finally, she said, "No, how could I kill my mother? George, I'm going to be a mother."

I stood stock still while I took it in. Then I realized the trap she'd set for me. Her mother was right, she was a tramp, and I told her so.

"But George…" she said.

"Get the hell out of here," I said. "You and your goddamn tricks. Get out, I don't want to see your face again." I pulled her out of the bed, thrust her dress into her arms and flung her at the door. She started getting dressed, fumbling at her clothes, and I opened the door and pushed her into the hall. Goddamn whore, getting herself knocked up like that. Let the neighbors see her for what she was.

Chapter 13

Summer 1967

"That's not how it works, you know," Alice says.

"You teach science, too?" I say. "I was a goddamn kid. What the hell was I supposed to do?"

"What happened to her?"

"No idea. Probably went home, then her mother shipped her out to Chicago or something."

"You never heard from her again?"

"No," I say. "I had other things on my mind."

"You were really on your own at fifteen?" Alice has put aside the medical tray and climbed onto the bed with me. She's curled against my side, one hand resting on my belly. For now, I feel safe as a kid in bed. I stroke her backside and smoke a Lucky.

"It's not like I was a schoolboy anymore," I say. "I had a job, my own apartment; I was an adult. Lots of kids were. We didn't have time for playing in the sandlot, you know." Except, I found out, Stooky did, hanging around the community center, learning to play basketball and getting preached at by the priests. He's probably got a mortgage, three kids, and a death wish by now.

"That still doesn't explain how you ended up in a road-house on the Connecticut border with your face looking like a tenderized steak."

"I'm getting to it, sweetheart. Gimme a chance."

"Tell me something that'll take me away from this dump."

"You don't know how good you got it," I say.

She grabs my dick and starts to play with it. "Is this where I find out how you went to jail?"

"How'd you know I did?"

"Teacher always knows," she says.

Chapter 14

Summer 1937

I still don't know exactly what happened, but it was fucked up real bad. It was a simple job on the other side of Beacon Hill. I met Vic Spruce, another guy from the Gang, in Boston Common and we walked a roundabout route past the State House to our target. We knew the family was gone; we'd seen them loading up the car for what looked like a long trip. It was summer, so maybe they were going to Hull or Cape Cod. It doesn't matter. All we had to do was get inside, grab what we could, and take off.

Beacon Hill is a quiet neighborhood. Vic and I wore rubber-soled shoes so we wouldn't wake anyone as we slipped through to Mount Vernon Street. Not even a cricket chirped.

The gas street lamps were the only lights we saw the whole way. We took a right off Mount Vernon and went into an alley behind the house. I boosted Vic to the window. It took about thirty seconds before he had the lock off and was pulling me up.

We were in the library, and the dark wood of the bookcases and paneling made the room absolutely black. I lit a match, just to find the door, and we went into the hall and upstairs to the bedrooms, where we figured the best loot would be.

The house was tall and narrow. Still, any of the rooms were big enough to fit all my furniture, and still leave space for dancing. I bet the chandeliers were real crystal, but there was no way to take them.

We found three bedrooms: one on the second floor, and two on the third. There wasn't much to take, just some small pieces of gold and silver, one emerald ring. Whatever they had, they must have taken with them, or left in a safe. A place like this, they were sure to have one hidden in the wall somewhere. Even if we found it, though, we had no tools to get into one. We went to the kitchen to see what kind of silverware we could cart off.

That's when we realized we weren't alone. The maid's room was next to the kitchen. As we walked by, I heard a girl's voice say, "Shh! What if it's the Mister? If he finds you, I'll be sent home for sure!" There was more than a hint of a brogue mixed in with the fear. A man's voice answered, "Don't worry, I'll take care of this."

Vic and I were ready when he came through the door. He was wearing only shorts and carrying a vase we'd heard him empty on the rug. I grabbed his raised arm and rapped it against the door jamb. The vase crashed to the floor, and at the same time Vic slugged the guy in the stomach. The poor bastard slumped to the ground, right on top of the shards from the vase. He gave a short scream and fainted. There's a man for you. The maid ran at us, hysterical, and naked to boot. She got off one swing before Vic slapped her across the face. He lifted her back to the bed and straddled her, putting his knees over her flapping arms.

"Let's go," I hissed at him, but he turned and grinned at me while he undid his pants.

"In a minute," he said. He slapped her again, then grabbed the back of her head and shoved her face into his crotch.

In general, I had no problem with Vic making a little extra score, but to be honest, I was thinking about Rose, and everything else was a blur. I should have ditched the whole thing and let Vic have his fun. Instead, I left the boyfriend on the floor and hurried to the kitchen to grab anything worthwhile. Nothing. I went back to the maid's room to get Vic, but he wasn't ready, he said. The boyfriend was starting to wake up. "Hurry," I told him.

"You can't hurry…" he started to say, then she bit him. His scream was worse than hers, a long, high wail that was sure to be heard by anyone nearby. Even as he fell backward, she didn't let go. He started to whimper. After a few seconds, he went limp, and she let him go, spitting blood in his face. I pulled him off the bed and dragged him to the front door, his pants wide open. He could barely stand, and I knew we weren't going to make it.

We hadn't gone a block when the police car pulled up next to us. They put the cuffs on me, and I was stuck in the car while they carried Vic and his bleeding cock into the hospital.

Within a week, I was already on trial for breaking and entering, burglary, and attempted rape. The last charge was because the D. A. said I would've done the same thing if the maid hadn't used her particular brand of self-defense. The jury bought it, and before Vic was taking a painless piss, I had already started serving five years at the Charles Street Jail. If I ever saw him again, I decided, I'd finish what the maid had started.

Chapter 15

Summer 1967

What I don't tell Alice is that the whole time I sat there in jail, I could see across the water to East Boston, where I knew my mother still lived with her new husband. My new plan was already on ice, but it just gave me more time to work out the details. That asshole Bricks was in charge now, I knew. Had been since he turned on my father, earning the dough that should've been mine. It would make it that much harder to get to *her*, so it's better that I didn't go off half-cocked. I needed to make the right friends, and you couldn't do much in this town without his hearing about it.

But with my new name and no white hair, if he ever heard about me, he wouldn't know I was Rico's kid. I stared out those bars at all hours, wondering what she was doing, how she could live with herself after killing my father and planning to do me, too.

It's after midnight, and Alice has fallen into a doze. I can feel the cut on my face oozing, and I try to slide out of bed without waking her. No such luck.

"Where you going?" she says.

"Gotta take a leak," I say.

"Where I come from, we say 'I have to go to the lavatory.' "

I laugh, but my words aren't so funny: "I'm not one of your junior high kids, you know. If I have to piss, I'll say so."

When I get back, she's wide awake again. "Get me something to eat," I say.

"Like hell. I spend all year looking after little boys like you."

I go in the kitchen and look in the icebox. There's some kind of casserole, a roast chicken that's showing some bones, lettuce, and a block of orange cheese. I take a drumstick off the chicken and bring it into the bedroom.

"Selfish bastard," she says. "What about me?"

"I thought you were going to sleep."

"Really, you are just like a little boy, you know that?" But she smiles and gets up and brings back a plate for herself. She has a couple of beers, too. More 'Gansetts. We move to the kitchen table, naked and hungry.

"What about you?" I say. "Didn't you ever get married?"

"What, and lose my job?"

"You never wanted kids?" As it comes out of my mouth, I don't know why I asked that. I see Liz again, dead and bloated, her legs open, the blood streaked like she was making a snow angel. I hear a voice, but no words. I force my mind back to the present.

"...Hard enough dealing with those children all day, I don't need to come home to another one."

"It's different, though, isn't it?"

"Not really. I read to them, put bandages on their skinned knees, clean them up when they get muddy, listen to their whining and cheering all day long."

"But they're not yours. You leave them behind at the end of the day."

"And go where?" she says, washing down a bite of cheese with her beer. "This town's about as big as a baseball field. I know everyone in town, and they all know me."

"Really?"

"Sure. I taught half the guys you saw in Sully's. They just stay away because it's too strange to have a shot in front of someone who made you memorize all the state capitals."

"Those punks?"

"Never would've hurt me," she says, finishing the square of cheese on her plate. "They'll stop by tomorrow, all red-cheeked, and ask if I got home okay."

I stand up, but my legs can barely hold me steady. "They know where you live?"

"Don't worry, they'll bring your car, too. They're really nice boys, just bored."

I'm kicking in the dark looking for my clothes. "You stupid bitch," I yell. "Stupid, goddamn stupid bitch. Do you know what you did to me?" They couldn't have gotten half a mile without realizing they were sitting in blood. The only reason they hadn't come here yet was that they were probably arguing about whether to go to the police or play the knights in shining armor themselves.

"What are you talking about? They're just joyriding. Jesus, weren't you going to stay the night anyhow?"

I'm dressed, and my head is throbbing. I pick up the gun and shove it in my front pocket. "Gimme your keys. Christ, I have to get out of here." She's huddled against the wall, trying to cover herself up with her arms. Whatever chance we had is gone. What the fuck was I thinking when I came here, that I could hide forever? Goddamn whore tricked me, like they always do. "Where are the keys?"

She's crying, pointing to the floor where she'd dropped them when we came in. That seems like a year ago. "You killed me," I say.

I run outside to the car. Somewhere I can hear engines racing, and I wonder if they're headed here. I get in the car, fumble with the ignition, finally turn the key. Nothing. "I'm a dead man!" I scream, turning and turning the key.

It's the starter motor, I know it is. I get out, jam my fingers into the grill looking for the hood latch. I cut myself good, and it takes me two more tries to find it and then lift the hood. By the light seeping out of the kitchen door, I find a stone and whack the motor a few times. I try again, and it turns over. I get out one more time to put the hood down, and Alice comes out, wearing a robe now. The distant engines are drowned by sirens.

"Will you tell me what's going on? What happened?"

"Just don't tell them anything. Give me that much, a head start."

She reaches out to wipe the blood from my face, but I push her away and get in the car. I throw it into reverse, skid out of the driveway, and aim into the darkness away from the growing sound of sirens. The last glimpse I get of Alice is her waving to me, her robe falling open.

But I don't get a chance to think about it. The engine roars and I put my foot to the floor. If I can get out of town, if I can keep moving, I might make it. As I skid into a turn, I can see red and white flashing lights in the rear-view mirror. They're pulling into her driveway.

I'm still driving in blackness, surrounded by trees. Somehow, I end up passing Sully's roadhouse again. It's after closing time, the lights are out, but the lot is half full with stragglers. I pray to hell they don't recognize Alice's Ford, but anyone going as fast as I am is bound to get noticed. As I go by, I think I see the two punks among the losers who can't get up the balls to go home.

Sure enough, a minute later, there's a couple sets of headlights blinding me in the mirror. Looks like at least one of the bikers is on my tail, too. I'm trapped, and the goddamn road keeps winding. At every turn I get closer to losing control. I'm struggling to get the .38 out of my pocket with one hand, steering with the other. They're staying right with me.

The damn gun is hooked on the edge of my pocket, and these curves are too tight, coming too fast. Fuck it, I need both hands, that bike is close enough for him to touch my rear fender. A tap of the brakes, a swerve, and that's one bike down. I see the parade I'm leading swerve around him. Looks like he took out one of the cars, too. But that's still a pair of cars and another bike. I might be able to make up some ground on this straightaway. Christ, it's like I'm at Daytona, but this goddamn Ford is redlining already, and those assholes aren't even tired.

The cars have moved ahead of the bike, and they're spreading out, one to each side, both in my blind spots. The guy on my left is driving in the other lane. A car's coming toward us, and he sees what's happening. He slams to a stop, dodging my wingman. Glancing in the mirror, I see him shaking a fist out the window. Come on, pal, what's your problem? You're gonna get home tonight, have a story to tell. Me? I'm running out of steam.

But they haven't caught me yet. The bunch of us slalom through a sleepy little town, all the storefronts dark except for neon signs throwing splashes of red on the street. We have to fall into single file to fit between the sidewalks. They're close enough for me to see three, maybe four, dark shapes in the mirror. Gotta get to that gun…

They beat me to it. The rear window opens up with a rain of glass on my neck. The shot echoes in the car, and I'm fishtailing, spinning the wheel any way I can, desperate to get back in control. The rear end slips out from behind me, and as it hits a parked car, the vibrations squeeze me like a giant fist. I can hardly breathe, my body feels like it's being shaken apart. My head snaps back and forth like a speed bag with bad rhythm, and I feel the *thunk* of a street sign getting mowed down. I didn't even realize I was on the sidewalk. I yank the wheel over, and the tires hit the street with a double jolt. There isn't a part of me that isn't suffering.

But I can't give in. I'm breathing fire, but at least I'm breathing and still going forward. As the front end straightens out, the tires grip the road again, and I jackrabbit forward. The one car that almost had me is a block behind, and then the town's a shadow in the dark. They fire another shot, but only the sound reaches me.

The impact shook my own gun loose, and it skitters across the seat. I can just reach it, and if I stretch my arm just right... Two quick shots out what used to be the rear window. Now they're skidding behind me, but I only hit the edge of the windshield. No damage done, dammit.

We've got some newcomers to the party, by the looks of the lights behind us. I can't tell if the bike is there anymore, but between these demolition derby drivers, I can make out at least two black and whites. Jesus, Ma, did an old betrayer like you stir up every demon in hell when I sent you there?

And now there's another pair of black and whites blocking the road ahead. Well, the only way you can find out your fate is by testing it. Last time, it landed me in the hospital, and my life almost turned around. Could it happen twice? Full speed ahead.

Chapter 16
Summer 1967

The Ford's headlights drill a hole in the dark, lighting up the two cop cars in my windshield like they're on a movie screen. One guy frantically waves his flashlight, like that's going to stop me. His partner scrambles out of the way, but these guys are used to chasing kids swiping candy out of the jar, not serious folk like me. Even in these couple of seconds, I see their old legs struggling to carry their weight to safety.

One car is parked straight across the road, but the other is at a slant away from me. I aim for that one, instead of trying to take them both out. If I can push it out of the way, or even put it out of commission, maybe it'll cause enough confusion before they pile into the other one like the Keystone Kops. I steel myself, gripping the wheel till I think it's going to crack. The sound of the engine fills the car, but I can just hear their shouts above it. The old flashlight cop is a bright blur against the dark a half second before…

Jesus Christ, that hurts. I think I blacked out a second, but I'm still alive. Hitting that police car knocked the rear of my Ford off the ground. I felt the impact over my whole body even before my head whacked … well, I don't know if I hit the wheel or the windshield or what. Then, when it started to come down, I felt like I was floating, like what those astronauts talk about on the television. They never said anything about tossing your guts out, though, and that's what I did, right before I bounced up and hit the roof.

It's quiet now, and everything's covered in puke and blood and glass from the shattered windshield. The smell is awful, but there's something else mixed in with it. I know it, I know it. What the hell is it?

Shit, it's gas. Gotta move. But my leg, which is it? The left, it won't budge. Christ, I think I shattered my knee. The door's hanging open; if I push with my other leg, I can make it to the ground and pull myself. Everything's so damn quiet, but I can sense other guys moving around me. They're not coming up to me, though. You think they'd have the balls to drag me away, even if it's just to put the cuffs on. Fuck 'em, one more shove against the floor and … Fuck! That hurts! But I got my arms working, and that smell keeps me going.

They're all on the shoulder on other side of the car. I don't think they're even looking for me. Just waiting for it to go. Push, push, drag. Slide across the street like a sidewinder, swing my one and a half legs back and forth. If I can put any weight on my left leg, I can reach the handle and get in the other black and white.

Jesus help me, but I did it. And they left the keys, too. I rattle my head, clear as much of the fog as I can. All it does is splatter blood on the dash and window, but I'm upright and moving again.

I pull back, and the rear of the car drops into a ditch in the shoulder. The jolt finds all the worst parts of me. Half my ribs must be broken, and maybe part of my left hand, too. Maybe now's the time to call it a day. Right, after all this. Fortune favors the brave, and all that. I slam the car into forward, and it lurches back onto the road. I gotta make a three-point turn to avoid the wrecks, and I can see the cops waving their arms, like that's going to stop me.

I'm finally facing the right way, and the old parade is

backed up behind the two totaled heaps. I'm starting to hear something, but it's still just a lot of shouting. I hit the gas, and I'm off. Screw it, for fun I'll put on the lights and siren, and head on down the road.

I haven't gotten half a mile before the gas in my Ford lights up. Suddenly, it's like daytime. Rich orange light fills the sky, and for a second, I see the shadow of my car stretched out against a building ahead of me. The strength of the blast behind me makes me think I'm about to follow it right into the wall. Before the light snuffs out again, I see the two cars, the Ford and the black and white, hit the ground. No one's standing, and the rest of the crew that were chasing me are at a standstill. I'm going to make it, I know I am. I turn off the flashers and siren and head into the darkness.

Chapter 17

Winter 1942

I got out of jail on February 13th. Friday, of course. But that didn't bother me a bit. It was cold that day, so the first thing I did was buy a paper to see what pictures were showing. Apparently it hadn't been such a lucky day for the Japs, because we'd sunk a bunch of their ships. Good, I thought.

For old time's sake, I thought I'd see what was showing at Keith's. *How Green Was My Valley*. It didn't sound like the kind of thing that would charm my snake, you know? But the Fine Arts Theatre was showing a double-bill, *Sins of Bali* and *She-Devil Island*. After five years in the can, that's what I wanted. I got on the trolley to the South End and had a fine time. Then it was time to get things squared away.

I had walked out of jail onto Charles Street wearing an old suit and holding twenty dollars in my pocket, all I had to my name. The twenty was enough to get me a flop in the West End, a part of town I'd never actually left, considering the jail was on the edge of it. I took the top floor of a tenement on Merrimack Street, looking directly into passing elevated trains. I didn't care much about the noise because my bedroom was in the back, and within a few days I got a radio to drown out the sound.

When I went in the pen, the Gang said they'd take care of

my stash, but since then there'd been a big turnover. A lot of guys got pinched, and nobody I talked to seemed to know what happened to my dough. I hadn't seen or heard from Vic since he'd gotten out of the hospital, but I'd made plenty more friends on the inside. I wasn't long without income.

I answered an ad for a mechanic at a garage in Cambridge, not far from my new place. It was across the river from Braves Field. I took the streetcar down Comm. Ave. to the Shell station with the huge flashing sign. After that, it was a cold windy walk over the bridge to the garage. The field is gone now, and they moved the sign across the river, but Billy Cooper's old shop is still there. No one remembers him, though. His kind get replaced every fifty thousand miles or so.

Billy was alone in the shop when I walked in the open bay door. He had on a greasemonkey suit, leaning against a green Buick Sedanette, smoking.

"What's it in for?" I asked, nodding at the car.

"You here for the job?" he said. "If you are, then you tell me. I don't have time for bullshit."

I shrugged, then walked to the other side and lifted the hood. He didn't get his ass off the fender, just leaned over enough to give me room, and kept smoking. I rooted around, not finding much. It was practically new. I poked the butterfly on the carb.

"Running rough, is it?"

"That's what the old lady says." I flicked the butterfly again, then got an oil can. Half a squirt.

"Now," Billy said. "The question is, how much do you charge for that?"

This was the real test. Anybody could fix a car in those days. I put down the hood, looked her over. "Old lady, you say?"

"Yup."

"Husband?"

"Died in the last dust-up."

"Where?"

"France."

Old widow driving a new Buick. She'd got on with her life, didn't seem too broke up about it. Who'd that remind me of? "I'd charge her for the labor, full overhaul of the motor and carburetor, two guys, the whole day, plus parts. Was she wearing jewelry?"

"And a fur stole."

She sounded like someone I used to know. "Make it three guys," I told him.

He gave me the job, though the cars driving around then were more complicated than the old jalopies I'd whipped around five years before. I learned my way around them quick, though, and soon enough I was a pretty good mechanic, with an even better sideline.

Billy was a good guy, always ready to lend a helping hand. He was big, about six-three, well over two hundred pounds, and I used to think he could drink twice his weight in booze and still not show it. One night we hit a dive near the garage, a small, dark place. We were the only ones in there, before the day shift let out at the factories. Hunched over the bar, with a shot glass hidden in his huge paws, he didn't need much to get him going on how he'd got his start.

"I did some work for James Curley back in the thirties. I was part of his campaign team, before he announced his run for Governor in '34."

"What'd you do?" I said. "Drive the car with the megaphone?"

"Nah," Cooper said. "I was more of a behind the scenes guy. See, one night Curley come to see me, walked right into my garage. 'Billy,' he says, 'Billy, I hear you were with me during the '29 election.'

" 'Yes, Mr. Mayor, I sure was,' I says to him.

" 'I appreciate it, Billy. I wonder, though, if I ran again, could I count on your help?'

"I told him, 'You bet, Mr. Mayor. I'll be with you as long as you need me.' That's the way he is, you know? No matter what, you want to be his friend. I told him, 'It sure is good to have you back home.'

"Curley says, 'As a matter of fact, I think I will be running again. There's only one problem.'

" 'What's that Mr. Mayor?'

" 'That damned Ku Klux Klan. They hate us Catholics, you know.' "

Now I know Cooper must be lying. I put down my drink and say, "The Klan? Since when was the Klan around here? I met a bunch of guys in Charles Street, but I never once met someone who admitted to wearing the hood."

"Just listen," Cooper told me. "Learn a little something."

I took a long pull of my beer. "Tell me," I said.

"Well, Curley says to me, 'Oh, they're here, Billy, m'boy. They're here. And they're going to get me elected.'

" 'How's that?' I asked the Mayor. Then he explained what he wanted me to do, and a few hours later, just before midnight, me and my fellow 'Klansmen' set up a cross right on Boston Common."

"You?" I said.

"Christ, George, shut up. Yeah, me and my friends, we put on the hoods and the robes. We set up the cross right in the middle of the Common and lit the damn thing on fire. Then we nailed a poster on a tree saying we'd drive Curley right out of Massachusetts."

"What good would that do?"

"Well, if the Klan was so afraid of Curley, then he must have been doing something right, you know? Then, he just *happened* to be walking through the Common with a couple of photographers, and when he saw that cross, he kicked the shit out of it. Those newspaper boys ate it up."

He laughed and slapped the bar so hard my glass jumped.

"Goddammit, if there weren't any Klansmen in town, he'd invent them!"

We laughed so hard the bartender must've thought we were a couple of school kids. "He's running again," Billy told me. "Now it's for Congress. I can't wait to see what he pulls this time."

Billy was a good guy, and careful. He waited a few weeks and made sure I knew what I was doing before he let me in on his scam. The garage was on a dark street not far from the river. There weren't any houses, just little factories and other industrial buildings. After business hours nobody drove by, except Billy's boys. He had a car-theft ring going through there, and when I came aboard, it was my job to strip the car down to a bare chassis, keep the best parts, and help load the rest on a truck bound for a friend's garage in some other town.

I got fifty to a hundred bucks for every car I stripped, plus a cut of the profits from selling the parts. At an average of three cars a week, within a month I was doing well enough to get out of the West End for good, and I moved to a decent place in Cambridge, right outside of Central Square. It was close to work, and something was always going on there.

I worked for Billy Cooper, but as he introduced me around, I made more and more contacts. It was like a Lions Club for criminals. If someone needed a wheel man, they called me. If I was looking for a partner in a B & E or a fence for some loot, there was this list of guys always looking for a score. Our only problem was that none of us was "connected" so we couldn't get too big without someone trying to horn in on us. The mob was mostly interested in gambling and sharking, but they weren't blind to other ways to make money. Every once in a while, a made guy showed up, but that's when I made myself scarce.

I'd changed my name, and for anyone who might have known me in the old days, I'd been dead for years. But I was still leery when I was working with a connected guy. That bastard Bricks was boss of the city by now, the position my father should have had. The one that would have been mine, maybe, by now. Just working with a guy that answered to that back-stabbing son of a bitch made me want to kill someone, and I knew just who that was: the woman who planned it all.

Chapter 18
Autumn 1942

I got through the war better than most. What with the legitimate job and all the rackets we had going, I was getting pretty rich. I had a nice apartment and plenty of girls tired of waiting for their soldier-boyfriends to come home. I figured there was nothing wrong with that — how many of our boys were diddling women in Europe? Christ, who wasn't? When I wanted some fun, I could get into any club I wanted. Sometimes I'd hit two or three in a night, usually with a different broad at each one. I was twenty-three, rich as a bastard, and ready to go. I tell you, those were the days.

There weren't too many clubs in Boston at the time, but the ones that were there were real joints. In Scollay Square we had the Village Barn, Orlandella's, Jack's Lighthouse. I liked to go to the Latin Quarter, down near Essex Street, too. Dancing all night long.

But of course, the best of them all was Coconut Grove. It wasn't Saturday night without a stop at the Grove. The Grove was where all the best girls were, and they were yours for a drink and a dance. Everybody went there — soldiers on leave, older couples, anyone who wanted a ritzy night out. They even set up this extra room in the basement, turned a storage closet into an extra bar and called it the Melody Lounge. It didn't have windows or anything, they just draped fabric from the low ceiling, and hung little lights from it, so once you fought your way down the tiny staircase and muscled into the room, you were under the stars.

Me and some of the guys would go down there late and act like we owned the place. You needed reservations to get in, but not us, even though it was always packed. We went often enough, spent enough money, that if there wasn't a table, the waiters set one up for us. We'd drink, meet some pretty girls, dance for a while. If the broad was really nice looking, we'd get our pictures taken with them. They loved that.

Then, one night, I saw *her*.

It was summertime, 1942. I hadn't been out of jail six months. I stood in a crush at one of the bars watching the show on the main dance floor. I got a cocktail for this dark-haired girl I was hoping to make. She was wearing a tight red dress that showed off most of her tits and barely reached her knees. I hadn't gotten her name, but the way she was looking at me, I could tell we'd be getting to know each other real good. The crowd was pushing her up against me, I could hardly move, and it was all I could do to keep the drinks from spilling. I noticed a little commotion on the dance floor, but I paid it no mind.

Then a sharp smell like fermenting peaches snaked its way into my nose. Suddenly, the girl in front of me disappeared, breasts and all, and I was six years old again. My mother's voice rattled in my head, screeching like a sick animal. We were on the sidewalk near our house while she yelled at me about embarrassing her in front of her friends. I felt the sting of her hand across my face and the snot filling my nose.

Then I was back in the Grove, looking over the girl's dark hair, and I saw the club's owner, not five feet away, shooing a half dozen banker types and their wives out of a huge booth in the area called the Terrace. All to make way for one couple.

Climbing into the booth, they looked like a pair of rats

curled up in a hole, their beady eyes scanning the crowd. I forgot about the schemes I had already thought up and started figuring a way to kill her right then. My eyes flicked to the exit, considered the likelihood of making it out alive. I didn't have a gun on me, but there was a chance I could vault the wrought iron railing and throttle her before anyone could stop me. Maybe cut her with a broken bottle swiped from the bar.

They were all bad ideas, and I knew it.

Instead, I took the chance to watch her, like a god in the clouds.

They were watching the floor show, a couple of dancers doing a tango. I was above and behind them, completely invisible, and I could stare without worry of getting caught.

Her face hadn't changed in the years since I'd taken that dive into the harbor. She was wearing black, like she should've been, but there were so many carats on her hands and neck that she looked more like a jeweler's display than a widow. Her wide hat was bright and cheerful. The waitresses were falling all over themselves to make sure everything was just right, but from the bored looks on their faces I knew Bricks Mancini and his wife couldn't give a damn. They just expected this kind of treatment. Then I saw her knock the tray out of the hand of a waitress who blocked her view.

That was enough for me. "Come on," I said to the girl. "Let's get out of here."

I took her back to my place and worked out my frustrations on her. When I was through with her, I called a cab and bundled her, bruised and crying, into it. I had work to do. From what I'd seen at the Grove, I knew that my idea of just walking right up to my mother and shooting her, maybe when she walked out of a shop, was a fantasy. I started to put a plan, a serious one, together. It would take time and careful preparation, but I covered every angle. I didn't sleep all night.

It was about a month later, around Thanksgiving, that the Grove burned down. I was supposed to go that night, but some of the guys wanted to see Rose la Rose do her thing at the Globe Theatre instead. It sounded like a good time, and I figured if I really needed to go for a drink afterward, what would stop me?

Rose always put on a hell of a show, even if you didn't really get to see anything. Not like my old Rose. When we got out, though, I remember the whole sky was lit up, like a sunrise or something. We didn't know what was going on, but word passed soon enough. A crowd snaked its way along the streets until the smoke stopped us about a block short of the club. Still, from where we stood we could see bodies everywhere. Ambulances came and went every minute, and fire engines had come from every town imaginable. I found out later on that Buck Jones, the cowboy actor, died in the fire. Everyone said he was living up to his hero image, saving people to the end, but how could anyone know for sure? I may have done some bad things in my life, but that night I cried.

When the war was over, Billy Cooper hit on a new way to make money. All those GI's were coming home, full of the American dream, just dying to spend some dough. He cut back on stripping cars and turned to selling used ones. He'd bring in these real shit-boxes and I'd fix them up till they were just drivable. If the gear boxes rattled, I poured sawdust in them. If they had too many miles, I'd crack the odometer and roll it back a few thousand. Simple stuff, but it brought in loads. And when some hot shot came in to complain, Billy showed him the fine print on the guarantee — it absolved the seller of any responsibility once the thing left the lot. It was beautiful.

I was making so much money, I used to wrap bundles of it in tin foil and put it in the back of the icebox for a rainy day. Hell, I could have bought my own ark during the flood with that cold cash.

It was about two years after the war that I bumped into a friend of mine from the Gang, Max Diamond. We used to call him "The Shiny Sheeny" because of his name. It didn't bother him, even the "sheeny" part, because we all had names like that. I was "Black Georgie" on account of the dye in my hair.

Max left the Gang just after I went away and took up on his own. He was trying to make a name for himself doing armed robbery. Basic jobs, like walking into a liquor store or gas station or any kind of place wearing a stocking over his head. He'd pull out a gun and take the cash.

When he saw me on the street, his eyes lit up.

"Georgie!" he said. He grabbed my hand with both of his. "I had a feeling I'd be seeing you. What are you up to these days?"

"A little of this, a little of that. You know how it is."

"Sure, sure. Say, you still in the business?"

"Why?" It was a long time now since we'd been in the Gang. More than one graduate had changed sides since then.

"I'm just asking, because if you are, I got a deal going that you just might be interested in. Whattaya say?"

"What do you have in mind?"

We went to a coffee shop near the Boston Garden, and he outlined his idea. He liked his stick-up jobs, but he was ambitious. "I want to do banks," he said.

"Banks is a big jump from liquor stores, Shiny," I told him. "You can't just walk in and take what you want."

"You think I have no finesse?" he said. "The way I have it planned, we don't need guns, or nothing. They'll give us the money with a smile and say, 'Come back soon.'"

"'Come back soon'?" I almost spilled my coffee.

"That's right. And we will."

It was too much. Whatever it was, I had to be in on it. It

sounded too crazy to miss. "OK," I told him. "If the teller asks me to come back, I'm in."

"Perfect. And by the way, don't ever call me 'Shiny' again."

We did our first job a week later. We started small, just to see if his idea would even work. Max and me and another guy, Al Sherman, drove out to Roslindale to a little savings bank. Beforehand, I'd gotten a make-up kit and painted us all up. I gave Al a good-sized scar on his chin, like he'd been in a car accident and hit his head on the wheel. I made Max look like a spic instead of a hebe, which wasn't too hard, he had such dark skin anyhow. All I had to do was add a tint of olive. Myself, I wore a bald wig that even Max couldn't tell was fake, right over my black hair.

Max brought Al in on the operation because he was a printer and pretty good forger. I didn't like it, the guy had no credentials, but Max was a stand up guy, so I had to go along. We needed Al to print up checks and money orders to cash. The scam was nothing more than cashing phony checks.

I went first at the bank in Roslindale. I brought a real check for something like a hundred dollars and cashed it. "Thank you," the teller said to me. Then the magic words: "Come back soon."

Al and Max waited in a parked car around the corner. When I came back, I told them the teller didn't do a thing, didn't even check my ID. So a few minutes apart, they each went in and cashed phony checks. I went to a donut shop nearby and had coffee. When no one was looking, I slipped into the men's room, took off the wig and make-up, and went back to the bank. All in all, we each made two trips to the same bank over two or three hours, and no one ever asked us a single question. Out of an investment of about two hundred dollars, to cover the real check and the make-up kit, we made over seven hundred bucks.

And all without a gun.

Chapter 19
Winter 1949

At the same time, I was still working with Billy. He'd opened up another dealership even though he had a record and couldn't do it legally. Instead, he was the "silent partner" with his eighty-five-year-old uncle, who didn't know his own name, let alone that he owned a car dealership. It was across from Braves Field and the Armory, where Boston University's football field is now.

Now that people were getting on their feet and getting somewhere, they didn't just want cars, they wanted new cars. And Billy was there to help. He would take in new shipments and sell them like nobody's business. He could even sell the same car twice. He often did, in a way. What he did was, when a guy bought on credit, Billy would send a second finance slip in to a bank other than the one the buyer had gone through and collect the payments twice. Or, in the rare event that some hot shot paid cash, he sent in the finance papers anyhow.

I'd been working with Billy now for six or seven years, and we'd done each other a lot of favors. So I figured he'd get me a good deal on one of his Fords, and he did. What I didn't figure on was that he'd finance mine twice like he did to the other simpletons who came in off the street. When the first overdue notice came in a few months later, on a car I bought with cold hard cash (it took an hour to thaw), I walked on the lot and practically gave him the bull's rush into his office.

"Billy," I said, "what's going on here? I pay for a car and all of a sudden I'm getting overdue notices?"

"Don't worry about it," he said. "I do it all the time."

"So? Don't you make enough dough without screwing a pal? I just wanted a nice car. You didn't even cut me in on the deal."

"Jesus, you're a greedy bastard."

"And what do I do when they come and repossess a car they never possessed?"

"You come back and buy a new one. By then you'll want a new car anyhow."

"I don't think so."

"What's the matter? You wanted a good deal, and I gave you one. You think I'm running a charity here? You know how it works. I do it to all the guys."

"Not me," I told him. "That's for the idiots who don't know better, who don't understand it's not their fault. You're going to fix this thing with the bank, because I don't care to have any of them breathing down my neck, got me?"

"*Got* you? Get *this*, pal. If it weren't for me, you'd still be doing hack work in some shit-hole, stripping stolen cars. Now you're a big shot, and this is the way you thank me? Go to hell. I got customers." He tried to walk past me, which normally he could have done, he was so big. But I was hopped up, and I grabbed a tire iron off the floor.

"Fix it," I said.

"Fuck you."

I swung the iron at him. It should've broken his arm, but there was too much beef on him. Instead, he grabbed the thing out of my hands, leaving a streak of rust and grease across my palms.

"Now what are you going to do, asshole?" he said. "Cry?

Get the fuck out of here. I have a business to run." He threw the tire iron to the floor, and it bounced with a clang. By the time I caught up to him, he was already on the lot feeding some poor chump a line about his excellent finance terms.

I don't know what I was thinking, but I jumped him from behind, and before he threw me down, I had slugged him a few times. The customer took off, Cooper laughed, and I wound up with a broken rib or two. I'm not sure, I never went to the hospital, just sat wheezing for a few weeks, trying not to move too much.

When I was feeling better, I traded the car in for a Dodge at another dealership. I paid the balance in cash.

After leaving Billy, I went in with Max and Al full time. We used that phony check gag all over New England. Just moved from town to town, mostly the rural ones in western Massachusetts, or up north where they didn't much expect to be taken. We always used different disguises, even lifts in our shoes to change our height. Once we finished a town, usually in about three or four days, we took off for a new one, at least a hundred miles away, and started all over again. We could make a few thousand dollars a week each, and never once did we use a gun.

But after a while, Max started itching to pull a real caper. "I know this was my idea," he said. "But it goes against my nature. I need something to make my heart rush, you know?"

So we tried a few old-fashioned hold-ups, like in the old days. No make-up, just white handkerchiefs. Max got his rush, but me and Al were disappointed. We only got a couple hundred total, and it just didn't seem worth the effort. Once Al's handkerchief slipped off his face, but thank God the store owner was kissing the floor at the time and was too scared to notice. When we got away, Al really laid into Max.

"This shit is for the birds, Max," he said. "We're goddamned lucky he didn't see me. I say we go back to phony checks."

"That's because you have no vision. This is just small stuff. Practice. I've got plans, you know. Big ones."

"What are you gonna do, knock over the Federal Reserve?" I asked.

"We'll see," he said. "Wait and watch."

By now it was late in 1949, just before Christmas. Al and I were having a drink at my place. Max told us he had some big news and to meet him there. When he came in, he brought the cold in with him, and I poured us all another shot.

Max didn't even take off his coat. He downed the shot, I poured another, and he sat down in an easy chair, the one I usually sat in when I was watching my new television. We were laughing at Admiral's *Broadway Revue* with Sid Caesar and Imogene Coca.

"OK," Max said. "This is it. I promised you a big score, and now I'm gonna deliver."

"It's about goddamned time," said Al. "It better be good."

"It's perfect. I say we'll take fifty grand, easy. Maybe more."

I whistled. "You're not fooling around. What makes you so sure we can pull off such a big hit and get away with it?"

"That comes later. Call it a late Christmas present if you want."

"From a Jew?"

"That messiah of yours was a Jew. Now listen, this is guaranteed foolproof."

"Enough of the promises already," I said. "Get to the point."

"All in good time. Give me another drink."

I gave him the bottle. After another shot, he put the glass on the floor and said, "You know the Statler downtown?"

"Sure," said Al. "Over in Park Square. We're going to knock off a hotel?"

"I've been watching it for weeks now, and I have the whole operation down to the second. It'll be easy."

"A hotel is going to have fifty grand just lying around?" I asked.

"Sure. Payroll, room charges, you name it."

"OK," I said. "We walk into this hotel, take the fifty G's and no one kicks?"

"That's the beauty of it. As long as you don't want to go down in history as having pulled the most daring robbery this city has ever seen."

"*Don't* want to go down in history? I don't get it," said Al.

Max smiled. "You boys want to be rich or famous?"

Al and I looked at each other. "Rich," we answered.

We took turns casing the Statler Hotel. From the week before Christmas on, we'd sit in the lobby as if we were waiting for someone, go make calls in the row of phonebooths, watch the shift changes, and when they carried the money upstairs. When we had it down pat, all we needed to do was pick the day.

Max decided on a Monday morning in the middle of January. My birthday, it turns out, but that's not why I didn't like it. Any moron knew too much could go wrong at a time like that. The regular guys might be out, snagging a long winter weekend. There could be snow. But the timing was one thing Max wouldn't budge on. "It's gotta be that morning," he said. "Or never."

The weekend before the heist was a busy one. I watched a wrecking crew take down the old Crawford House in Scollay Square, one of the first joints to go. Some other guys pulled a robbery and kidnapping in the North End. I thought that would put the cops on alert, but Max said that only made things better for us. I was getting real nervous about this, so much so that I almost went to see Billy Graham the night before at Mechanics Hall, just to calm my nerves. But I didn't see any point in prayer. I just drank and watched television instead.

Monday morning, eight-thirty, Max and Al met at my place and we drove a Ford I stole in Chelsea over to the Statler. We parked behind the hotel, on Columbus Avenue, and walked around to the front. We were wearing nondescript clothes, all gray. Just before we went upstairs we put on masks made of paper bags with eye holes cut into them.

We had timed it to reach the office just before nine o'clock, before the secretaries showed up, before the cashier, manager, and guard brought the money bags in to the cage.

We jimmied the door and waited for them inside the office. When the door opened, Al grabbed the first guy to come in, the cashier, and pushed him to the floor. I pulled a club out of my coat and slugged the guard. The manager was laughing. He thought the whole thing was a gag at first, but when Max aimed a gun at him, the laughter dried up quick. We took the two money bags they'd been carrying, and then Max told the manager to unlock the cage, where another, bigger bag was sitting on a table.

I clubbed the manager and we put all three guys into the cage and locked it. We still had another three minutes before anyone was due to show up, so we closed the door behind us, cut through the ballroom to the exit on Columbus Ave., and jumped in the car. We were blocks away before the three were found, and by the time the police were called we were already across the river.

In all, we got just under the fifty grand that Max had promised, almost half of it in cash. We made the headlines in the evening papers; it was one of the biggest hauls in the state in months. "Don't get too excited," Max told us. "Remember that Christmas present I promised you."

Ours was the second big robbery in a few days. The police crawled through every back alley looking for a break, and the three of us split up after counting out the dough. Even though we'd pulled a clean job, had ditched the car behind a supermarket, and no one could finger us, we couldn't be sure what was about to happen. Simply because we all had records, they could pick us up, just on suspicion of knowing something. And as it turned out, I did get hauled in. But it had nothing to do with the Statler heist.

It was January 17, 1950. I had just gotten out from seeing *Deadly is the Female*, with Peggy Cummins. She's this carnival performer who does shooting tricks, and when she meets this nice guy who loves guns as much as she does, she marries him. But he doesn't make enough money for her, so that bitch drives him to a life of crime. It just shows what kind of trouble a woman can be to a good man. I liked watching the robbery scenes. They reminded me of how good a job we'd pulled. Outside the theater, I almost got hit by a pair of police cars screeching by like drag racers. A minute later, Boston lit up with flashing lights. The sirens sounded like air raid signals. You'd think we were getting bombed, they blew so loud.

I got home and turned on the news to see what the hell happened, and before the picture came into focus, two uniforms nearly put their fists through my door. They burst in, all blue coats and brass buttons, lifted me right out of the chair and bounced me down the stairs into the snow. I wasn't wearing a coat, and only had slippers on my feet. Every guy ever convicted of anything got dragged in, anyone with even a juvie record, anyone who knew someone with a record. They had us stacked like that in every police station across the city. It was like a Who's Who of Boston felons, a parade of both nickel-and-dimers and big-timers. And there I was, with no coat and wet feet, looking like one of the losers. But we all had one thing on our minds: was someone in this hallway the guy that just pulled the Brink's job? Word was that crew had taken almost a hundred grand. Later, the papers said it was closer to three million, half of it in cash.

They pulled us into the rooms one at a time, like priests calling old ladies into confession, only no one was talking. My detective, sweating despite the winter wind coming in the open window, pounded me hard about a similar robbery a few years before in Hyde Park, but I was clean. Next thing I knew, they let me go, and I was out in the cold in my wet slippers again.

Max was right. The heat was off of us. The newspapers even said that compared with the Brink's hold-up, ours was amateurish. There were no worries that eventually the Statler culprits would be picked up. What they really meant was they considered us small-time, and had bigger problems to deal with.

And so did I.

Leaving the police station, I grabbed an evening paper to read on the subway ride home. Almost the whole first page was taken up with the Brink's story. Then, in the bottom corner, I noticed that one suspect in particular had been taken in for questioning by the Special Services Squad themselves — that bastard Bricks Mancini, the alleged head of the Boston Mob. They had a picture of him with his wife, Carla. There she was, my darling mother, in a photo from the society pages, not a bit of mourning black to be seen on her. She had completely forgotten about me and my father.

But somehow, someday, I'd remind her.

Chapter 20

Summer 1952

We kept a pretty low profile after the Brink's job. The police and Feds were everywhere. I found out that within an hour of the heist, they raided two houses just outside of Boston based on pretty slim tips. Just thinking about the heat made me sweat on a cold night. I didn't talk to Max or Al for months, and we waited a long time before we spent the dough we'd gotten. Too many people were on the lookout for big spenders. As it turned out, one of the best leads they got on the Brink's job was a ten-dollar bill spent in Maryland, for God's sake.

I got myself a straight job working at a garage in Somerville. It was slow and boring, but it kept me out of trouble. Max and Al had some plans, but I passed. They tried luring me back with bigger cuts on the action, but I was doing pretty well at the garage, and after a year I had two guys working under me.

I wanted to keep my nose clean. I had more important things to take care of.

Finding out where my mother and her husband lived wasn't hard. It was in black and white right there in the newspaper. The problem was trying to put any kind of a tail on her. I couldn't just sideswipe her while she was crossing the street. They lived in the North End of Boston now, right near Paul Revere's house, and the neighborhood never slept. It was common knowledge that Mancini gave good rewards to any one of his neighbors who passed along decent tips. No one, not even the Feds, could crack the place. Everyone from kids to grandmothers acted as spies, watching out for any strangers at all.

I'd gone down a few times, drank espresso sitting by café windows, hoping to catch a glimpse of either of them. But I only saw her once, from a distance across the street. She was surrounded by goons, buying — probably just being given — what looked like a roast at the butcher.

It had been almost ten years since I'd seen her at the Coconut Grove, but she'd still hardly changed. Only a few gray hairs showed that she'd aged at all. But she did carry herself differently now. When she was married to my father, she already seemed old and bent, and stared at the sidewalk when we went to the market. Now she jutted out chin, sharp enough to put an eye out, if anyone got that close. A lane opened up for her on the crowded sidewalk, and no one dared look straight at her. She was a proud bitch, wearing a fur stole and diamonds to the goddamn butcher shop. I forced myself to sit calmly until her bodyguards helped her into her car and drove off. Then I stood up to leave, and I only realized how angry I was when I knocked a table over.

I kept up my vigils, but it was useless. Sometimes I'd see a big black Cadillac speed through the streets, and from the way everyone got out of its way I knew one or both of them were in it, but that was all. I didn't dare ask any questions.

About the same time, the Kefauver Senate committee made the news, announcing that a syndicate was operating in this country, and Boston was one of its main bases. It shouldn't have taken some Senator to figure that out. But everyone was jumping on the bandwagon, trying to play Eliot Ness. Now that Hoover had to do something about it, the G-men were trying to blend in by eating at Italian restaurants, splattering their white shirts with spaghetti Bolognese. Whenever I saw them, I had to keep myself from laughing.

I didn't laugh long, though.

I'd been straight for almost two years. I hadn't heard from anybody in my old life in months. Then one night I went out to a club down the street. I had a few drinks while I watched the dancers, thinking I'd like to get one for myself for the night, when someone slapped me on the back. I turned around, and there's my old pal Shiny Max.

"You looking for some of that?" he said, nodding towards a dancer. "I know a place."

"Max, how the hell are you? What've you been up to?"

"This and that. You busy?"

"Do I look it?"

"Sure you do, playing pocket pool. Come on."

He took me to a brownstone in the South End, down Columbus Avenue from the Statler. It didn't look like much on the outside, but once we got through the door, it was like a con's wet dream. Girls in silk robes and silk stockings, girls drinking booze and smoking, girls in high heels flirting with guys on plush red chairs, girls getting felt up and loving it. One pointed to Max and whispered something in her friend's ear. They laughed.

An older woman met us at the door and smiled at Max as if she'd known him for a long time. "What's new, big boy?" she asked him.

"My friend's been out of the game and he's lonely," he said. "Who's feeling good tonight?"

The madam turned and waved around the whole room. "You like blondes? Marie over there is something special. She's worth two all by herself."

"I'll take her," I said. "And that one over there. I always had a thing for redheads."

"That's Colleen. Hey, Colleen! Marie! Show this gentleman up to room seven."

"I'll pick up the tab on this one," said Max. "See you in the morning."

"Aren't you going to have a throw?" I asked.

"I'm going to have a talk with Sandra here," he said, putting his arms around the madam. "We have a few things to discuss. Have a good time."

Colleen and Marie took my hands and we went upstairs. The room had a king size bed in the middle, with silk sheets and a mirror on the ceiling. Marie sat on the bed behind me, and unbuttoned my shirt, while Colleen undid my trousers. When she had them off, she opened her robe and dropped it. Her body was covered with freckles, and I planned on getting a taste of every one. While I worked her over, Marie watched with her hands between her legs, getting herself ready. She sure got her share of me, too.

I woke up late the next morning. The girls had left. I dressed and went downstairs. The parlor was empty, but the smell of cigar smoke and whiskey was as strong as ever. I heard voices in the room in the back and followed them into a small kitchen. Max sat with Sandra drinking coffee. "How was it?" he said.

"Great," I said.

"Colleen can really clean your pipes, eh?" said the madam.

"I'll say."

"Well," Max said. "Have some coffee. You had your fun last night, now it's time we talked business."

Sandra poured another cup and gave it to me. "What's on your mind?" I asked.

"What d'ya think?" he said. "I need a wheelman. Feel up to it?"

"It's been a while," I told him. "I've been on the straight and narrow."

Planning a bigger score, but I wasn't going to let him in on that.

"Hey, I did you a favor. So, you going to be my driver or what? I told Sandra you'd be a stand-up guy. Don't make me out to be a liar, Georgie."

"Bumping into me wasn't an accident, was it?"

Sandra glanced at Max, and it wasn't friendly. He patted her hand, but she just grimaced more. Then he looked at me and said casually, "Not much of one. I saw you at the service station a week or so ago, thought you looked bored. I got a sense about those things, you know."

"Bored" was the wrong-sized wrench, but he was in the right toolbox. "Like I said, what's on your mind?"

Max smiled, and Sandra's face lightened up. "I knew you'd see it my way. Didn't I tell you, Sandy? George is a stand-up guy. Here's the deal. We're going to hit the Five Cents Savings Bank, near City Hall. I've got it all worked out. It'll be just like old times."

"Like the hotel, or like our old M.O.?"

"A little of both. Look, there's no risk. With this one job, we'll be all set. Then I'm going to take Sandy on a long trip somewhere to California or Mexico and live free and easy."

"Don't you have anything left from the Statler score?" I asked.

"Things have a way of drying up. Know what I mean?"

I did. I'd gone through my stash, too.

"How much is my share?" I asked.

"I thought we'd split it sixty/forty. I'm the one going inside."

"Fifty-five/forty-five," I said. "I have to make it through the traffic."

Max bounced his head, as if he were figuring in his head. "OK," he said. "It's a deal."

"When do we do it?"

"Next Friday morning, after they bring in the cash for payday."

The morning of the job, I boosted a Chevy from a house in Cambridge, outside of Harvard Square. I picked up Max a few minutes later and we drove straight to the bank, crossing the river by the Longfellow Bridge, waving a salute to the guys in the Charles Street Jail as we came onto the Boston side. We pulled up against the curb a few doors beyond it, near City Hall, and Max walked down the hill. I opened a newspaper and pretended to read it while I watched for cops. No one bothered me, and I was starting to get pretty confident when Max came running back to the car. He jumped in the back seat, just yelling, "Oh, shit! Shit, shit! Oh, shit!" I looked back to see he didn't even have a single bag with him.

I put the Chevy in gear and took off down School Street. I could already hear the sirens, over Max bellowing, "Oh, shit! Oh, shit!"

"What happened?" I yelled. "Tell me you didn't kill anyone!"

I whipped the car around the corner onto Washington Street, heading to Roxbury. We'd follow the rest of the plan and ditch the car there and take the elevated from Dudley Street. Back then, it was a Jewish area, and Max picked it because he'd feel at home if we didn't make it to the trains. These days, the Jews've all moved out and it's starting to become a ghetto.

Max was crouched down in the back seat. A single police car followed us, and I prayed the Chevy could outrun him just long enough to get us to the elevated, before the rest of the cavalry came in.

He finally caught his breath. "A total washout," he said. "As soon as I reached for my piece, this Geronimo of a guard took a shot at me. No warning. I high-tailed it out of there damn quick. Man, it was just like he knew I was coming."

We were under the elevated tracks, with the cops still on

us. I darted under the stations at Dover and Northampton Streets, but there was no shaking them.

"Who else knew about this?" I wove in and out around the traffic, until I saw another cop coming straight at me. "Who knew?"

I whipped the car around to the right, trying to duck down a side street, but the goddamn thing skidded out from under me. The last thing I remember was Max saying, "Who do you think?" and me realizing that Sandra was the rat. Then the car flipped from under us and the roof collapsed against one of the elevated supports. I heard the screech of the cops slamming on their brakes. Then it was black.

When I came to, there were leather restraints on my arms, and both my legs were in casts, hanging in the air. It didn't take long to figure out what the restraints were for. I was pretty sure a cop would be standing outside my door, just dying to arrest me in my bed. Goddamn bastards. I pulled once at the restraints and gave up. It wasn't like I was going to escape — my broken legs were throbbing and my head hurt so much that just opening my eyes was torture. But soon a pretty nurse came in and saw me awake, and a minute later I was face to face with Captain Mulcady of the Boston Police Special Services Squad, one of the sweating shnooks I'd met the night of the Brink's job. Six weeks later, I was out of the hospital, and six months after that, I started my fifteen years at the new Walpole State Prison.

Chapter 21

Summer 1967

I enter a wooded area, heading north. I'll be back in Massachusetts soon. I can reach the Turnpike. I haven't been down here since … well, since it opened. Just a couple of jobs out that way before I was on ice. Now it's up to six lanes, they say. That'll be my best shot, US 90 all the way to the west coast.

First, though, I have to keep my mind on the road in front of me. Even though the cop car handles nice, it seems the pavement keeps shifting underneath me. I blink blood out of my eyes, but it's so damn hard to see. I'm telling my arms and hands and foot to work, but I can't actually feel them. My left leg is just dead beneath the knee. I'll have to find a doctor before too much more time, but…

"Wake up!" *My mother's voice.* "Wake up!" *she says again. I can't have been in bed long, but now she's in my room, dragging me by the arm.*

"Mama!" I yell. "That hurts!" Of course it hurts, I got the cane today for talking back to the teacher. Now she's squeezing my swollen fingers. "How could you do that to me? Don't you ever embarrass me like that again!" She grinds my knuckles again, rolling them against each other, and it's like the bones are exposed, scraping and cracking.

"Stop! You're hurting me!"

"*I'll show you hurt!*" *She bends them back until I think my hand will snap off. My arm is paralyzed, and bolts of pain shoot into my toes. I'm crying now, loudly, so Papa will come save me, but if he's let it go this long, he must not be home. I scream again, and she lets off a string of curse words, a mixture of Greek and Italian.*

"*Who do you think you are? Every time you open your mouth, you make me look bad. Is that what you want? And then that slut of a teacher thought she could tell me something about raising my own boy!*" Alice? How could Mama know about her, I'm only six years old, I…

"*…Wake up!*" *she yells again, but I'm not in bed, I'm looking her in the eye. I see Mancini on the ground, but she doesn't seem to notice him.* "*Wake up, you stupid little boy. Where do you think your father was all those nights? Who do you think gave you everything you had? You think* he *did? He was off playing cards and robbing honest shopkeepers' tills. You think because he gave you a dollar or a story, he was some kind of hero. I'm the one that kept you fed, who made sure you had a reason to come home every night, even if your father couldn't be bothered. And now you put a gun in my face, and kill the one man who actually loved me?*"

"*You were already sleeping with him before Papa died.*"

"*Like hell I did. Where do you get ideas like that? It was your father who betrayed you, not me.*"

"*Don't lie to me, not when it's the last thing you're going to say.*"

Then she does it. The most disgusting thing I can imagine. She reaches to the top of her dress and rips it open. Her tits are hanging there, wrinkled and limp. I can barely look at her. But I can't look away, either.

"*I nursed you until it hurt. When your father left us both alone, I stayed. You never went hungry. I gave you my whole life, and this is the respect you give me? I'm your mother!"*

"My mother! All you ever did was make my life miserable."

"Miserable? If I ever made your life hard, it was because he *was never there to make it easy. I raised you alone, and any strength you have you got from me, not him. Go ahead, murder your own mother." She stands up straight, thrusting her shriveled tits at me.*

"You're the murderer, not me," I say. "You killed yourself."

And I shoot her, right through the heart.

"…Wake up!" But this time it's not her voice. It's rougher, a man's voice. Familiar, too. Papa? No, not him. Who? I can't open my eyes. My hand's on fire. I try to move my fingers, but they're nothing more than broken sticks, jagged and splintered. Flaps of skin stretch and break around them. It must look hideous.

"George! Wake up. Hey, Georgie." That smell. I know it. Not gas. That was … when? This is sharper. Cleaner. Alcohol. Like a doctor's office. How did I get here? Hands on my leg, probing my smashed knee. Everything hurts so much, it doesn't matter.

The clink of metal on metal. A scalpel on a tray?

"You killed yourself," I say. Who's listening? Who's dead? A slap on the cheek, but I still see only darkness. More metallic clatters. Glass? Didn't a windshield shatter? When?

"Blackie! Black Georgie! Remember me? Dammit, snap out of it, wake up!"

Max? Max Diamond? Who else calls me Georgie?

Another voice. Old, frail. "He's in shock. Let him come around on his own, if he can."

"I don't have time for that, and neither does he."

My hand again. Poke, poke. *Shit!* He's shoving the bones right back in. *No!* But it goes on, and I feel the bones rolling under his fingers as he tries to fit them back into what's left of my hand. One slips under the a tendon…

…Another slap, and my eyes pop open. I see light, but nothing else. Looks like from one bright light in the ceiling. Then, before I know it, my stomach seizes. Feels like my head will pop open, but it goes out of my mouth, must've been the lining of my stomach, because I've hardly eaten anything since … when? That mustard sandwich? In that dark attic. What was I doing there?

"Christ, Georgie, those are new shoes you just ruined."

"Max?"

"Now you're talking sense. Jesus, you gave me a scare."

"Stop taking the Lord's name in vain, buster."

He laughs. "He ain't my God. My people only recognize the original, not that sequel you *goyim* worship."

It's Max, all right. "You never see someone for the last time, do you?"

"You got that right, Blackie. And lucky for you I'm the one that caught up to you. Those other bastards were like to skin you alive. Another minute, I wouldn't'a been able to tell you from a wet spot on the street."

It must be gauze over my eyes. I see the dark of his face in front of the spotlight, but nothing else. "Where the hell am I?"

He pats me on the shoulder, and for a second I think I'm going to pass out again. "I got you to the first sawbones I could find. This is Doc Alsdale. He's gonna get that hand stitched up in no time, aren't you, Doc?"

I hear a shuffle behind me. "Well…"

Max squeezes my shoulder, and the bolt of pain makes me yelp. "Aren't you?"

"There's so little to work with…" Alsdale says. "I never did this kind of work, and in my office … he needs a surgeon."

"Well, my friend isn't going to get to a hospital, not tonight. Some serious heavies are out to kill him, and they're going to be haunting the emergency rooms looking for him. When they realize he's not going to make an appearance there, they'll do the same thing I did, and you know, it wasn't hard to find you."

Alsdale doesn't say a word, but I hear him turn and open some cabinet doors. "Don't worry," Max says. "You're in real good hands. I can tell this guy has seen some shit in his day."

"How'd you find me?"

"You know me, Georgie. I got like a sixth sense. I can see things two minutes before they happen."

"So how'd we get pinched that time?"

"I don't always use it. Now shut up. Alsdale's almost ready. Don't worry about the scars, Doc. It'll make him look tough." There's a splash of cold water on my hand. I feel it working its way inside the wound. A half second later, it's burning, then it all goes numb. I hear a series of clanks, as Alsdale puts his instruments on another tray.

"Don't worry," says Max. "A couple more minutes, and you'll be right as rain. I got a sixth sense. Trust me."

I wish I could, but I know my friend Max from way back, and I can see the future, too, sometimes. I don't like what I can see though this gauze.

Chapter 22

Summer 1958

Fifteen years is a long time, but I kept busy and stuck it out. Walpole was new, and for a prison, comfortable. When the riots began, a couple of years before I got out, it wasn't so cozy, but that was long in the future for me.

For the first few years, I kept mostly to myself, stayed out of trouble. My first cellmate was Phil Carlisle. He kept to himself, too, but I found out later it wasn't really his choice. Everyone stayed away from him. It wasn't that he was tough. Actually, he was kind of a loser. He was doing time for accessory to murder, but he'd never pushed the button on a single guy. The problem was, his legitimate job made him a jinx.

When I was brought to my cell, he was sitting on the top bunk, reading a girlie mag. His legs hung down, swinging back and forth. The guard slid back the bars, and I stepped in, carrying my prison-issued sheet and blanket.

"Hiya," he said when the door slid shut. He held out his hand and I took it. It was strong and dry. He introduced himself with a voice as deep and smooth as a church organ. "I hope you don't mind the bottom. I hate to be down there."

"Why?" I said. "Rats?"

"Naw," he laughed. "They go where they want." He laughed again.

Phil was about thirty, and his hair was black and shiny, a natural version of my own dye job. His skin was pasty, and the smile he wore seemed forced.

"So what's the problem?" I asked.

The guard was still behind me in the corridor. "Go ahead, Phil, tell him. Tell him what you used to do." He laughed, too, and walked away, his chuckles lost in the taunts prisoners shouted at each other. The guard rapped the bars with his stick and told them to shut up.

"That's Norton," Phil said. "He's one crank you should make friends with."

"I'll bake him a pie," I said. When it looked like Phil had forgotten about me, I told him, "Well, get on with it. What's your deal?"

Phil's forced smile became a sincere grin. "I used to be an undertaker," he said.

"What's so funny about that?"

"Nothing," he said. "Good money in it, too."

"So what'd you do?" I threw the sheet and blanket on the thin mattress and started making up the bed.

He grinned. "Nothing," he said again. "I just know where the bodies are buried. All of them."

"Of course you do."

"No," he said, putting down the skin mag. "Not like that. I had this deal worked out with a few button men. When they needed to plant a body, I arranged it. All they had to do was bring the stiff to my father's funeral home, and I put it in with whatever I had going out the next morning. I had these specially-done false-bottom coffins. Designed them myself."

I stopped with the bed and looked at him. "Didn't anyone notice? I mean, the pallbearers must have known they were carrying the extra load."

"Have you ever carried a coffin?" Phil asked. I shook my

head. "Have any idea how much a coffin weighs? If anyone asked, I told 'em the box was heavy-duty. But hardly anyone ever did."

"So what happened?"

"I made a mistake once. I put this two hundred pound guy in with an old lady, must have been about ninety years old. I don't know what I was thinking. One of the pallbearers pulled his back lifting up the casket. And to make matters worse, one of her sons was a retired cop. Right there in front of everybody, he opened the casket, knocked on the bottom, and that was it."

"They won't forget that funeral for a while."

"The funny thing was, there was nobody to plant her. My father was out of town, and I was the only other undertaker. They had to put her on ice for a day or so before they found someone else to do it."

"So, what does that have to do with sleeping in the top bunk?" I asked.

"You figure it out," he said, and went back to his magazine.

Doing time was slow, but I kept myself busy. I was never much into politics, but I found out quick that the cranks will leave you alone if you help them out. I never caused any trouble, and I was able to set up my own little auto shop. I was giving tune-ups, changing oil, that sort of thing, for just about every guard, and even the warden once in a while. I did good work, and I never took any money for it. I liked making it look like I was just being friendly, handing out favors left and right. I made a lot of friends that way, and you can never have too many friends in the joint.

Once, when I'd been in for about a year, I got myself in a scrape in the shower. There were seven or eight other guys in there with me, but I noticed that one by one they walked out, some with soap still covering them. Before I knew what was happening, this clown about twice my size came in. He was hairy all over, and he took the shower right next to mine. I'd heard about the queens on the inside, but I didn't know he was one of them.

He smiled in a way I didn't like, and I rinsed myself off. I turned off the shower, grabbed my towel, and started to walk away, but he grabbed me from behind, wrapping that hairy arm of his around my waist.

"Don't be in such a hurry," he whispered in my ear. "We can get to know each other."

"I'll see you in the yard, if you want to know me," I said, and tried to squirm my way out of his bear hug. He pulled me closer, and I could feel his cock behind me. I tried to kick him, but I slipped and brought us both to the floor. He still had his arm around me, and I was on my hands and knees with him behind me. I couldn't move, and was having trouble breathing. His shower was still running, the spray falling on my back, running between my legs. His breath was getting quicker behind my ears, and he spread my legs apart with his knees. I made one last lunge from him, but ended up flat on my stomach.

"All right," he said. "This is gonna be the best fuck you ever had." With one hand he pressed my back into the floor, and with the other supported himself. I pistoned my legs, but all it did was scrape my knees against the tile.

I didn't notice the squeak of rubber shoes on the tiles until they were right in front of me. It was the crank Phil told me about, Dave Norton, standing in front of me. Before he said anything, he pulled back one big boot and cracked the guy on the head with it.

"Hey, Louie," he said. "What's the story? That boyfriend of yours get some class and shut you off?" Norton kicked him again, and Louie rolled off of me. I scuttled over to the wall and used it to steady myself as I stood up. Norton gave

Louie a few more whacks with the boot, and the hairy queen took it without a squawk.

"Go on, George," said Norton. "I think Louie and me are gonna have a private conference. I'll talk to you later. By the way, since you changed the plugs, the Chevy's been running great. Mind if I bring in my brother-in-law's Ford sometime?"

Like I said, you can never have too many friends in the joint. I did that car, and about six others, on a regular basis for Norton, and I'd still be doing them today if I knew where he was.

A week after Phil got released, a guard came and opened my cell. "You got a new friend, George," he told me. "Treat him nice." He closed the door and walked away.

He was skinny kid with a twitch in his left hand. He threw his stuff on the top bunk then turned and leaned on the bars, trying to tell how far he could see down the corridor.

After a few minutes I said to him, "Got a name, kid?"

"Yup," he said.

"Well, we're going to be here a while," I told him. "We might as well get to know each other now. What else are you going to do? Stare at the corridor all day?"

"I won't be here long," he said. He couldn't hide his fear. "It's all a mistake. As soon as my lawyer explains it to the judge, I'll be walking on out of here."

"When'll that be?"

"Any minute now."

"You keep twisting your hands on the bars like that, maybe you'll wear them away and we can both walk out of here. Come on, kid, haven't you done time before? What's your name?"

"Don't matter." A door slammed somewhere, and he jumped expectantly. He practically shoved his head through the bars thinking it was his lawyer. When he realized it was just another con being led back to his cell, he slumped to the floor.

"Better get used to it," I told him. "This could take more than a few hours. What happened?"

He sat on the floor across from my bunk and rested his arms on his knees. His left hand kept twitching, the fingers and wrist bouncing to a rhythm I couldn't hear.

"It was an accident," he said. "If he hadn't grabbed the gun in the first place, it never would have happened. I just needed a few bucks to buy something for my girlfriend."

"What'd you knock over?"

"Liquor store."

"Imaginative. So you asked for some cash, and instead he tries to grab the gun, huh?"

He spread his arms out, glad that somebody finally understood. "Exactly. I didn't even think there were bullets in the damn thing."

"Of course. You shoot lefty?"

"Yeah, how'd you know?"

"I can read people," I told him.

His name was Marty Kaufman, and it was a week before the kid realized he was going to do some real time and settled down. He'd killed the store owner the first time he'd ever pulled a job. And his girlfriend never once came to visit him the four years I knew him.

Marty was a good-looking kid from Everett, about twenty-two or -three when he came in. He was thin and had blond hair — a perfect target for the queens. Even though he hadn't done anything for me, I let the cranks know he was a friend of mine, and to keep a lookout for him. He didn't know he had a guardian angel, but I never once heard he'd been bothered.

Everett's not too far from Boston, and I asked him about news from the street. I told him I used to know the boss, Bricks Mancini, but that I hadn't heard much from him lately.

"You worked for him? Jesus, that's the big time. You ever kill for him?"

"No," I said. "I never did that. Armed robbery is my strong point." That puffed him up. Here he was, locked up with a mobster, or so he thought, and he's the one that's in for murder. He thought it made him important.

"So what's he been up to?" I asked.

"I don't know," he said. "I never really hung out with that crowd."

"Well, you must've known someone," I said. "How'd you get the gun?"

"This kid I knew from the corner. Everyone knew he could get whatever you needed."

"What about the boss?" I pressed. "Don't you know anything about him?"

"He's still around," said Marty. "I think he moved to the suburbs, though."

"With his wife?"

"I guess."

"Where'd he move to?"

"I don't know. Dedham, I think."

"That's right up the street from here."

"Yeah, I guess you're right," Marty said. "Maybe he'll come visit you."

"Maybe," I said.

I didn't sleep well that night. I heard Marty crying to himself for a long time before his sobs finally became snores. The bastard Mancini was still running the show, conveniently close to my new home. My back yard, if I could take a walk. I knew it was still years before I'd get out, and a lot could happen. But the thought that he and his wife were in spitting distance kept coming back to me.

And the time went by slow and steady.

Chapter 23
Summer 1967

"We haven't got all night," Max tells the doc. "Put the stitches in now."

"The stit…?" But Alsdale stops. Someone is holding my injured right hand above my head. With my left, I pull the gauze off my eyes and stare Max in the face. I barely recognize him. His grimace is what I see first. I notice that he's gotten thinner, and his famous curly black hair has gone limp and gray.

I scan the doctor's office. Dark paneling, leather-bound books neat on the shelves. On the oak desk in front of me, there's an electric iron sitting up like a dog, a long black cord snaking out from behind. Next to it, an Army Captain's hat and a pair of spats, the kind the Great War vets wear in the Fourth of July parades, which, it occurs to me, is in a couple of weeks. Spats. I spin my head and catch a glimpse of Alsdale.

The first thing I see is the fear in his pale blue eyes. His head is completely bald, the skin stuck to his skull like a weathered poster on a billboard. The needle in his hand shakes, and it's so big, I can practically see up the tube.

"Do it now," Max shouts, and Alsdale plunges the thing into my good shoulder.

It doesn't knock me out, but I feel like rubber. Max holds me upright as I slump against him. Then I feel his grip, as strong as it ever was, on my wrist. It doesn't hurt, so whatever Doc Alsdale has given me must be working. My tongue is thick, like I've been drinking. The room won't stay in one place. When I turn to look at Max, my neck almost snaps back. I pull it forward, and my head flops to my chest.

Something is on my arm. Tightening. A noose. No, a belt. On my arm? Who's the drunk one here? Don't they know what they're doing? But when my eyes take in the saw in Alsdale's hand, I sober up real quick.

"Hurry," Max shouts, straining to hold me still. I can feel the pressure of a scalpel slicing through the skin on the back of my hand. My words won't come out. I sound like Boris Karloff in *Frankenstein*, howling incoherent grunts, but I'll be damned if I don't snatch my wrist back before he grabs that sawblade I see in the tray.

Max has got hold of the belt, and Alsdale's grip on my shattered hand tightens some more. He's not even trying to be gentle. I can't feel the pain, but I *can* feel the broken bones and tendons rubbing against each other. He's stronger than I would have expected. As much as I writhe, my arm stays in place, flaps of skin peeled back, exposing the bones.

Then the blade is on my wrist. It looks like a miter saw. Doc looks at Max one last time, and I see in his eyes he doesn't want to do it, but Max barks, "Now!" and the saw rasps through the bone. Every tooth seems to catch and rip, and a cloud of bone dust puffs up off the blade. It's the worst pain I've ever known, until he pulls it back and goes deeper. Three more strokes, and in a gush of thick clumpy blood, it's off. I can't hear anything over my own screams, but I see Alsdale whisk the hand, *my* hand, off the table and into the chipped white enamel pan. Did he have that on the battlefield, somewhere in France? How many times had he done then what he's just done to me?

Then it's the searing pain of the iron. Christ! A bolt of pain flies up my arm, then down to my balls, shriveling them to raisins. He's cauterizing me with a fucking iron! The smell of burned skin and boiling blood fills the little room, and I see even Max isn't prepared for it. He's making sounds like he's retching. Through the tears in my eyes, I can barely make out Alsdale's movements, stitching the flap over my stump and wrapping it in what seems like a mountain of gauze. Despite the tourniquet, every layer soaks through with blood before the next turn.

Max is crushing my head against his chest, shouting in my ear like a mother soothing her babe, but I'm not a babe, and he's no mother, and this is no scraped knee. My hand is gone, my right hand is lying like a dead thing in a metal pan. My hand is gone.

Max is shouting in my ear. He's a thousand miles away, but I think I can hear some of what he says. "That's what you get," he says. "That's the price you pay." But it's all gibberish, and I wail for the loss of my hand, and for Liz, and the baby, and I wail for my mother and my whole fucking life.

Chapter 24
Summer 1967

I wake up stretched out in the back of a car, my wounded arm taped vertically to the passenger headrest. I'm packed so tight, I can't avoid puking on my arm.

"Thank God you're awake. I thought I was driving a hearse here."

I still can't form words, so I give Max another blast of puke. I'm not sure, but I think there's a hefty dose of blood coming up with it. I don't have anything left anyhow.

My hand is throbbing. No, I don't have a hand. It's phantom pain, like those old-timers talk about. Is that what I have to look forward to?

"Don't worry," Max says. There's a strange burst of static and mumbled words from his radio. "That doctor's not talking to anyone. And I took … took *it*. So no one's going to get your prints from it."

I groan some more. "What the hell are we going to do with a severed hand? For Christ's sake, you should've just torched the old doc's house."

In my mind it makes sense, but I guess it doesn't to Max. He just nods and says, "We're going to make it. Don't worry. I got a sixth sense about this kind of thing."

The stench of the puke clears my brain a bit, and I try again. "How'd … find … me?" is all that comes out. It's enough.

"I got one of those police radios. It's been going crazy since you popped Mancini. Hasn't been a quiet second all night. I figured that car fire in Providence was you, too. I was only a step or two behind you most of the night. Tell you the truth, Georgie, you tore the gates of hell right off the hinges tonight. You're goddamn lucky I caught up with you before anyone else did."

I take a second to process this, then try talking again. "Wha' 'appened?"

He glances over the seat. "You mean the road block? I almost caught up to you at that dame's house. You made the right decision, leaving when you did. Another second, they'd have dragged you from that broad's bed, with that uncircumcised dick of yours still dangling in the breeze. I had to hold back behind the parade you were leading, but I knew you'd need my help eventually. I saw you get thrown, then climb into the police car before the whole place lit up. It nearly burned my eyes out. I drove around the whole mess, and no one even saw me. When I found you wrecked a few miles on, I pulled you out and took you a couple of towns over to the good doctor. When they get around to looking for you, they'll spend hours thinking you're on foot."

Old Max, always looking out for me.

"Where're we goin'?" I croak over the radio static.

"We're almost back in Massachusetts. I know a place near Springfield. A quiet little motel. I'll stash you there until you're stronger, and we can figure out what to do next. Want me to get you a girl?"

He's driving smart, pushing the car, but not enough to call attention to us. He's in a heap of trouble just talking to me, let alone taking me across state lines. If he gets pulled over for anything, he'll be an accessory to how many murders, and they don't make any distinctions about who pulled the trigger. For what he's doing for me, my friend Max is looking at the chair, and here he is cracking jokes. Thank God there's still some loyalty left in this world.

Blood runs down my arm, pooling in my elbow, flowing down to my neck and chest. My shirt's drenched and clammy. I don't know how the hell he's going to get me into that motel room. But Shiny Max always comes through. He hasn't let me down yet.

"Just like old times," he says. "Last I saw of you, we were making a quick getaway."

And I ended up almost as bad as I am now. What ever happened to that rat Sandra anyhow? I know Max ended up out of state, some trouble with a sheriff in the south he never bothered to tell us about. It's a miracle he showed up when he did tonight. But the car bucks onto a road with potholes every few feet, knocking the thoughts out of my head. A few more lurches, and the rocking of the car wrenches my arm free. It smashes against the floor and suddenly everything lights up and Max screams, "Sorry!" but the damage is done. The stump throbs and threatens to burst. I have to lift it up with my left hand, the damn thing won't work anymore, it's as limp as a dead snake, but maybe, I think, maybe it's just the shit Alsdale pumped into me. God, let it be that.

Max has the car on a steady keel again, and we're moving faster. I float in and out of consciousness, and I have the sense he's slowing down now. I see streetlights flashing above me, first in a whirl, then one at a time, then farther and farther apart. Another minute, and the flashing red of a motel sign tells me we're safe. He drives around to the back and stops.

"I'll be right back," he says. "Don't go anywhere."

"Where'm I gu … go?"

"There's a topless bar across the road, for starters. Just sit tight."

He slams the door and another shot of fire goes up my arm and down to my balls. I'll never get it up again.

I don't know how long he's been gone, but Max is back, opening the rear door by my head. "Sit up," he says, grabbing me under the arms. I can help him a bit, scrabbling with my feet until they hit the pavement. That's when I remember I busted my knee, too, but I can't be bothered about it now. I'm dizzy, but I'm mostly able to get to the door he's pointing to. Together we stumble like drunks to the room, me leaning against the doorframe until he gets the key in the lock, and as we jerk through, the door slams against the wall. Max kicks it shut and says, "In there." He hefts me over to the bathroom, and puts me in the tub. "Now you can bleed all you want." He clears the rack of towels and dumps it on the floor next to the tub.

"Geh s'more," I tell him. "An' ice." Another bloody bathroom, the second this week. I left Liz lying there, and I don't even know if they've found her yet. It's been… what, three days now? They must have. Will Max do the same to me? I know I would've ditched a guy like me, but he's gone through the trouble to get me here in the first place. Still, can't depend on him to get me out of this. I have to trust to myself.

I start wrapping the towels around my arm, and when it's as good as I'm going to get it, I try unbuttoning my shirt. It's tough, using just one hand, and my left one to boot. It's like my fingers don't even know what to do. Finally, I figure there's no saving the shirt anyhow, and I yank it open. The dried blood sticks like glue, and I have to peel it off. Then I reach over to the faucet, get it going, and mop a towel over the worst of the mess.

For the first time, I can see what I've been through in the last few hours. And I'm not out of this yet. It's got to be two or three o'clock, but it's still deep dark out. How many dead tonight? While I'm trying to count, Max comes back with an armful of towels and sheets. I turn away to hide how relieved I am to see him, make it look like I'm tending to one of my many wounds. "Just raided the maid's closet," he says. "I'll be back with the ice in a second."

There's a mound of linens next to me, but it's that ice I really need. The end of my arm is burning; I just want to plunge that goddamn stump into something cold, something numbing.

"Keep it cold," Papa says. "It'll keep the swelling down."

"It hurts."

"That's good. It means you hit him hard as you could. That's my boy."

"Mama's gonna be mad I got blood on my shirt."

"You leave that to me," he says. He takes the pick and hacks a few more chunks from the block in the icebox. My hand is in a saucepan, and when he covers it with the ice, it both burns and freezes.

"What about my face?" I have to breathe through my mouth. My nose is clogged with blood and snot. I don't tell Papa I cried when that Irish kid got the first punch in.

He says, "I'm afraid it's going to be as ugly as ever. Molto brutto." It makes me laugh, but that hurts more, and a few more tears come out. He slaps me.

"Wake up," Max says, standing over me. "You'll have plenty of time to sleep when you're dead."

"T'anks for … 'couragement." My mouth is working better. I'm starting to think I got a chance again. Max is sitting on the edge of the hopper, holding a bucket of ice. "Put 'er there," he says, and it's all I can do to move my arm towards it. Without any squeamishness, he pulls the soaked towel off it and digs a hole in the ice cubes to fit it in.

"You'll be able to tell the broads this is your dick," he says. "They'll be lining up."

I manage a smile, but now it's time to think of more pressing matters.

"Can't stay long," I say.

He nods. "I know. I wanna make sure you're strong enough before I leave you for a little while. I need to torch that car. You bled something awful. I'll leave your … I'll leave the evidence in there. Too bad, it was a good set of wheels. Need anything else?"

"I'm good. Not goin' anywhere."

He stands up, fishes in his pocket for the keys, then says, "You gotta tell me, though. How did you get so close to the old man?"

" 'S a long story," I say.

"Spill it, brother. We got a lot of catching up to do."

So I tell him the whole goddamned story. Everything except that last, horrible week. Who knows how much of it makes sense, how much is morphine-gibberish. But it comes tumbling out of my mouth mixed with spit and tears and blood.

Chapter 25

1965

There in our cell in Walpole, Marty gave up on waiting for his lawyer and told me everything about the Boss. We settled into the routine of doing nothing. Then the warden announced a new program aimed at rehabilitating us. Some group of idealistic kids had the notion that what we needed was a little culture. If only we cons knew what we'd missed in art class, we'd be productive members of society. They came in wearing black berets, carrying easels and paintbrushes, guitars, and an armload of scripts. We felons were going to put on a play.

When we stopped laughing, we started jockeying for a place in the program. It may have been bullshit, but it was something different, and maybe there'd be an angle to it that someone could work. And if someone got to work an angle, I wanted it to be me.

Running the auto shop earned me the good will I needed, and one afternoon I found myself in the small library sitting in enforced silence, a raft of guards watching twenty cons while these kids talked to us about the benefits of artistic release. I'd never been up here before, this tiny room with a few wooden bookcases. There were a lot of legal books, but plenty of old dime novels and magazines, too. It was the only quiet place I'd seen here, away from the furious screaming in the cell blocks, the roar of the dining hall, the constant din of men who had killed and were ready to do it again. So I was happy to listen to them, if for no other reason than to have a minute of peace.

They showed us slides of prisoners' paintings that had brought in real money, told how old bluesmen learned to play in jail and got recording contracts the minute they walked into the sunlight. These soft little babies seemed to think that just by putting on a performance for the other prisoners we'd somehow change our ways. It was certainly bullshit, but one kid kept my interest.

There were five of them, three boys and two girls. They all had long hair, boys and girls alike. I wanted to drag those faggots down to the barber and give them a proper crew cut. Cut off their beards, too. But the girls were all right. One was blond, with a blouse much too big for her. I knew the other cons in the group would be thinking about her tonight, slapping themselves silly. But my eye was on the brunette. She had hair parted in the middle, twisted in thick braids that sat on her shoulders, like a squaw from an old western. She seemed older than the others, more sure of herself. She didn't talk down to us like the others did, like we were some kind of freaks, something to be afraid of. It didn't seem to occur to her that we were a bunch of burglars and rapists and murderers. Her voice was like one of those folksingers on the radio.

When the blabber of the longhaired boys dried up, she stepped right in. "We thought a long time about what kind of play we could do," she said. "We read a lot of different ones, and argued like you wouldn't believe. Some of us thought you'd like Shakespeare, something bold like *Macbeth* or *Henry V*. Others thought some of the Theatre of the Absurd would be more to your taste, Pirandello or Ionesco. I was pushing for the angry young men out of England, maybe John Osborne's *Look Back in Anger*. Maybe you saw the movie with Richard

Burton." She realized that we probably hadn't even heard of it in here, but she recovered quickly: "Anyhow, that one had too many women's parts." All of the names washed over us, but we laughed with her at the thought of a bunch of us in dresses. Louie would've liked it, if he'd been able to join us.

"In the end," she said, "we agreed on *Death of a Salesman*, by Arthur Miller. You might have heard of him. He was married to Marilyn Monroe before she died." Another mental picture that would get a lot of play tonight. I myself was thinking of Marilyn's skirt blowing up.

That was it for the day. After passing out copies of the play and promising to be back the following week, the kids were hustled out of the library and we were brought back to our cells. I ignored Marty and got to reading. I wanted to make a good impression on the Indian princess when I saw her again.

The next time the kids came, we had all read the play. I liked the way the wife stuck by her husband the way she did, no matter what. I figured I could play the lead, Willy Loman. I felt like he did, beat down by life. I could play him, or maybe his friend. Either way, I was sort of excited. It reminded me of the old days, with Stooky and Rose, watching *Cimarron* on that big screen, thinking I could be old Yancey Cravat, doing anything I wanted. It reminded me of Rose herself, and I imagined Stooky as the son, finding us in bed. He never did, of course, but it was just the same as if he had.

The first thing we did was divide up the group between actors and stage crew. It turns out, there were more guys who wanted to be behind the scenes than in front of them. "I'd rather swing a hammer than dance in front of those animals," said one guy, an armed robber named Gene Tully.

"Lookit the shy boy," laughed Frank Conners, who was doing time for assault and battery. "Me, I don't care what the fuck those punks say." I had no problem getting the part of Willy. And that meant I got to work with the Indian princess, who was directing the show. Her name was Elizabeth Murray. "Call me Liz," she said, but the crank shook his head.

"It would be better if they called you Miz' Murray," he said.

She shrugged. "So call me that." But we started right in calling her Liz, and the guard knew he couldn't stop it.

The stage crew went with two of the boys and the blond girl to a room that had been converted to an art studio, while the other boy stayed with the cast. Besides me and Frank, there were eight of us for almost twice the number of roles, so a bunch had to double up. After Liz assigned the roles, we started to read through the play. Some of the guys could hardly read. I was okay, but stumbled over a lot of the words myself. Liz wasn't bothered in the least. She corrected us on the hard words, let the little mistakes go. She had some kind of authority, talking the way she did to us, that kept us in line without rubbing our faces in it.

After an hour, we'd read through the first ten pages. The other kids came back to the library with a guard, but without the stage crew. It was time for them to leave. She nodded and said, "That's great for the first day. Get started memorizing your lines, and we'll see if we can get through the whole thing next week." Now it was back to real life for me, but I had something good to think about for the next seven days.

I almost blew it that night, though. I was in line for the slop they called dinner, when I heard one of the guys from the stage crew talking to his buddy about what we'd done.

"It's a bunch of horseshit," he said. "But I'll find a way to taste that director's sweet cunt before it's all over." My arm swung out, and the tray caught him right under the chin. His eyes bulged and soupy mashed potatoes flew everywhere. There was a scuffle, and after I got two quick shots in, I made sure he was getting the better of me when the guards got to us. "That crazy son of a bitch!" I yelled. "What the fuck did I do to him?"

He tried to sputter something about me, but no one listened. One guy said, "It's true, George here was mindin' his own, and Geronimo there just went at him." I got a night in solitary for fighting, but it was worth it. The other loser got pulled from the program.

The kids kept coming, one afternoon a week, for the next couple of months. I found out Liz was a nurse, and the boy who joined her, Mike, was still in school, studying history. She was older than the others, twenty-eight. Once we started getting our lines down, Liz and Mike worked with us individually, teaching us how to put some feeling into the words. Liz said to me more than once, "You're a natural at this. You missed your calling." I didn't tell her I'd been acting all my life, I could do a stupid school play. But still, I couldn't complain about how she smiled, and she was doing a good job with the others, too: it started to look like we were actually going to put on a play.

After about two months of sitting in the library, Liz was helping me with one of the long speeches, and we were both tired and getting frustrated. We had set a performance date for less than six weeks from then, and I kept forgetting lines I knew stone cold. But she just pretended it was nothing.

"You're an angel," I told her. "A regular Florence Nightingale." She blushed, and it looked nice framed by her Indian braids.

We forgot about the play, and under the eye of a guard we talked for a while. I was good about keeping my hands by my sides, but it was tough. She seemed honestly interested in me, and asked me all kinds of questions. I concentrated on her face, and the way she smelled. Clean.

"Did you ever do anything really bad?" she asked.

"I'm in a maximum security prison, and you want to know if I ever did anything bad?"

"I mean really, really bad," she said. "You know, like killing someone." I'd seen girls like her before, getting a charge out of being with a bad boy. It made them think they were being dangerous.

"What would you say if I did?"

"I don't know," she said. "Try me."

"Sorry to disappoint. The worst thing I ever did was the failed bank heist that put me in here."

"And now you're done?"

"Well, I'm pretty much out of commission. It's hard to do much behind bars."

"I'm glad you're not a hardened criminal," she said, dropping her hands to her knees. The sound drew my attention, and when I looked, I saw the outline of her legs through the thin material of her skirt. "I'm glad you're not a killer."

"What does it matter?"

"I'd hate to see someone as nice as you get mixed up in that. What'll you do when you get out?"

"Probably go back to fixing cars, that's all I'm really good for."

"Everybody's good for more than that. Especially if you're good with mechanical things. You could start your own business, support yourself."

"When did you become an expert on supporting yourself?"

"I joined the Peace Corps when I first became a nurse."

"You mean in Africa and all?"

She nodded. "I worked at a hospital in Ghana for two years, and taught people how to work for themselves. I saw it happen with folks who have a lot less than you do."

"Well, then," I said. "Maybe I'll start my own business when I get out."

It was time for her to leave, and after checking to see how close the guard was watching, she brushed her hand on my shoulder. "If you put your mind to it, you can do whatever you want."

I got in line with the other prisoners and watched her go,

trying to remember what I'd been like at her age. I'd lost that kind of idealism long before then.

Show time arrived. For the last two weeks, we'd been rehearsing not in the library, but in the small auditorium where sometimes we got to see movies. The blond girl was doing our make-up, and the other guys put up a fight about it. But when I happened to mention that a knowledge of disguises had served me well in my past life, they smiled and let her do as much as she pleased. The set, built and painted in the woodshop by the other half of the group, was up and ready to go. The families of the actors and crew were invited to watch, but I had no one to ask but Phil Carlisle, and he'd never volunteer to step inside those walls again.

The show went off okay. We forgot a lot of lines, and it was more like we were hamming it up than putting on a real show. I broke down laughing a few times, especially when Frank Connors, doing his first scene, froze like a rabbit in the road. But Liz, calling from behind the curtain, gave him his line, and we kept going.

I did miss out on one opportunity, but by then, I didn't care. Despite the fact that the family members were segregated from the prisoners, there was plenty of smuggling going on. From the stage I could see fidgeting hands passing cigarettes and other packages. The next day in the yard would see surge in bartering and fights.

I had a better deal, though. The warden had already given the go-ahead for another production, which meant I'd be seeing Liz again. And even though rioting in the cellblocks cancelled the program, I still I had a steady visitor to look forward to. My few minutes of happiness, once a week.

Chapter 26
Summer 1966

I was forty-seven years old when I stepped out of Walpole with a hobo pack slung over my shoulder. I didn't have to worry about my birthmark anymore — the white was hard to see in all the gray. Liz picked me up in a little brown VW Bug. I stood on the gravel outside the gate, taking in the sight of her leaning against the car. She wore a long blue skirt and sandals, and one of those too-big blouses. With her long Indian braids, she looked like innocence itself. But when she wrapped herself around me, I knew there was a little devil mixed in with it. I slipped my hand under her blouse but she twisted away. "Not here," she said. "It's a straight shot to my place. You can hold it in until we get home." I smirked and we climbed into that tiny car of hers.

"I feel like a clown stuffed in this thing," I said. "I had more room in my cell."

"Maybe you want to go back there, then?" She had a way of taking my shit without getting in a twist about it. I liked it.

Walpole is south of Boston, and Dedham, where Marty told me my mother was living now, was in between. Marty, poor kid, his lawyer never did spring him. But he was far from my mind as Liz and me drove along Route 1A, until it led us into the middle of town. After we passed a huge wooden schoolhouse and fire station, I told Liz to pull in to get some gas.

"What for?" she said. "I have almost a full tank."

"I gotta make a call."

"To who?"

"A friend of mine. Relax, I'll just be a minute." I ran across the street to a phone booth and dialed the operator. I asked for Peter Mancini's number.

It took a second, but she came up with it. "Let me just make sure it's the right one," I said. "What's the address?" She gave me that, too. I thanked her and went back to the car. "We have to make a detour," I told Liz. I gave her the street and told her to ask the attendant for directions.

It was a sleepy street, near the train tracks and a playground. The houses, some of them nicer versions of the two-families in old East Boston, had yards big enough for swing sets. A place for happy families. We drove past my mother's house, and I had Liz pull over at a house farther along the block. I pretended to knock on the door, while I checked out my target.

Their place was the biggest around, standing behind a small yard raised about five feet above the street, the only one set so high. Except for that, though, it hardly seemed the place for Boston's boss to live in. I was surprised not to see a fortress protected by goons who'd check out passing cars and pedestrians who got too close. Why would a guy like that live in a pink house, and would he or his wife sit on one of those porches that wrapped around both floors? I saw an attic window, and I thought that might come in handy later on.

I stopped knocking and went back to the car, making my plan. From what I'd seen, it was the kind of place where families knew each other and had coffee together and borrowed cups of sugar. I thought, this'll be a cinch. All I had to do was hole up in that attic for a little while, wait for the right moment, and whack them both. Maybe smother them with their own pillows, sneak out in the dark and be done with it. By the time anyone found out, I'd be long gone and happy.

I got back in the car and we left.

"What was that all about?" she said.

"Looking up an old friend."

We drove all the way through Boston, and I craned my neck out the window, taking in the skyscrapers they'd put up over the old railyards in Copley Square, with more on the way. She drove over streets that hadn't even existed last time I was here, but none of it fazed her. I pointed out where my old haunts had been, but she had no idea what I was talking about. Never even heard of the Coconut Grove. She was living in a whole new world that had nothing to do with mine. I thought, this could work. I thought, when I take care of what I need to, maybe I really can start over again.

Liz's apartment was in one of two high-rises that had been built over the West End, what would have been about three blocks from where I'd lived, a hundred years ago. It looked over the river, and you could see the Charles Street Jail, too, next door to the Mass General Hospital. She had moved there hoping to be close to work, but ended up working at City Hospital across town. "I like the view," she said. "So I'll stay here anyhow."

She parked in the garage and I took my pack from the stupid front trunk. The whole thing would crumble in a crash. I thought about the solid things I used to drive and wondered what the hell was happening in Detroit.

We stepped to the elevator. Liz lived on the tenth floor. Before we got to the third, I had my arms around her. Nothing under that blouse but skin. We got to her door, and she fumbled with the keys. When she opened it, I threw my bag on the floor.

"This is the living room... "

"The hell with that," I told her. "Where's the bedroom?"

She pointed with one hand, and I carried her to the bed. She scrambled out of my arms, and, dancing on the bed right in front of the open blinds, pumping her fists up and down, she tossed her blouse off. I took her feet out from under her and dropped back on the bed, and the skirt ballooned up around her. I reached in and pulled off her panties while she giggled like a schoolgirl.

I stripped off my shirt and shoes, and dropped my trousers. She reached into my shorts and pulled me towards her. I was inside her almost immediately. She gave a shout, then had her arms and legs around me, feeling me everywhere. I gave her everything I had.

It was dark by the time we finished. Her braids had come loose, and her wild, tousled hair hung over her face like a veil. I lay on my back and she was next to me, caressing my chest. Then she reached across me and opened a drawer in her nightstand. She took out a small bag. "Ever smoke pot?"

"You're into that stuff?"

"Why not? Just because I'm a nurse? Come on, you're not that old." She lit the joint, took a drag and passed it to me.

"No thanks," I said. "But go ahead, it doesn't bother me."

"Oh, George, it opens your mind! It's so good after sex. Actually, during sex, too. Just try one hit." She offered it again, and I took it.

"Aren't you a little old to be a hippie?" I asked. "I thought that was just for kids." I took a drag and started coughing.

She laughed. "Not so much! Just take it easy, like this." She took it back, and showed me. Her eyes were already turning red.

"I think I'll take a shower," I said. "Where's the bathroom?"

She pointed it out. "There's towels in the closet." I got one and closed the door behind me. I took a long shower, scrubbing the sweat and prison smells off me. It had been too many years since I'd felt this clean. Afterwards, I looked in the medicine cabinet and found a razor. I wasn't the first man ever to come in here. Whoever it was had left some shaving cream, too.

When I came out of the bathroom, wearing one of Liz's robes, she'd finished her joint and fallen asleep. She was curled up naked, clutching her pillow. The room was hazy, and the sharp smell of the marijuana made me dizzy. On the other side of the bed, I saw a sliding door that led to a small balcony. I went outside, leaving the door open to air out the room.

It was towards the end of June, and warm enough to be outside in just the robe. She had a folding chair in one corner, and I sat in it, looking into the night.

I could see straight down the river. On one side, the Cities Service sign glowed in the lights of Fenway Park. Farther down, on the other shore, I could just barely see the flashing yellow Shell sign near my old garage. It looked like they'd moved it across the river. It was getting on towards ten o'clock, and Storrow and Memorial Drives, framing the river, were nearly empty. Closer to home, I saw the State House with its golden dome, and just below me, an all-night drug store and the prison. I felt sorry for the guys on the inside, but then I remembered Liz huddled up in bed, and forgot about them. I went back inside, leaving the door open a bit to let out the rest of the smoke, and crawled into bed. Liz wrapped herself around me, and I fell asleep.

I woke early, expecting to hear the prison bell ring, and for a moment forgot where I was. Liz was still asleep, but during the night she'd rolled away from me. I left her there and went into the kitchen, looking for something to eat.

For the first time, I really saw her apartment. It was small, but plenty of light made up for it. The sun streamed into the living room through huge windows. She had these weird African masks and spears crossed all over the walls. Her only furniture was a small dinner table and a beat-up couch, the upholstery turning a moldy brown. A Hi-Fi took up most of a little table next to the couch. That was it.

I checked the kitchen. Not much in the way of breakfast stuff, but I'm easy. I ate a piece of stale cake, then boiled water for instant coffee. I went back to the bedroom to put on my pants.

Liz had woken up. She pulled her hair out of her eyes and smiled. "You're up early. What time is it?"

"Seven," I said. "Want some coffee?"

"Uh-uh. I don't have to be at work until eleven. Come back to bed."

"I can't sleep."

"You don't have to."

Just then the kettle began to scream. "Come on," I said. "Get up and have a cup with me."

She put on her robe and sat at the table near the windows, which had a better view of Beacon Hill than the balcony did. I poured two cups of water and spooned in the coffee. Slipping into domestic tranquility didn't seem all that hard. We were going to be like John Garfield and Lana Turner in *The Postman Always Rings Twice*: an old con and a beautiful woman making a go at being normal.

She watched me fumbling with the coffee and said, "You're doing it wrong. First the coffee, then the water."

"Does it matter?" I asked.

"I suppose not."

"Then shut up and drink it."

"Yes, sir. You know, I haven't slept that well in a long time."

"You must've been tired," I said.

She smiled. "I wonder why."

"There's plenty more where that came from."

"Well, finish your coffee and prove it." She untied her robe and stood up, letting it drop. I took her right there on the floor.

"Do you do this with all your patients?" I asked her afterwards.

"Only the ones I think I can save."

I got dressed. It wasn't the danger that turned her on, it was the idealism.

Chapter 27
Fall 1966

Liz kept talking about what I'd told her, when we first met working on the play, about opening my own shop. But it took almost a month before I could find a garage that would take me on in the meantime. I ended up in a little place near City Square in Charlestown, not far from the Bunker Hill Monument. I could walk there in a few minutes. I told Liz that I didn't want to waste money on the bus so I could save up for my own garage someday, but it was really because I liked to be outside, able to move, walk, cross the street when I wanted to. After fifteen years in the can, I needed all the freedom I could get.

I thought I'd have a hard time dealing with Liz, but it wasn't bad. Pretty quick we fell into a routine that kept us both happy. She worked a lot of hours, and when she got home she was too tired to hassle me about opening a shop. I was on my own as much as I wanted, and if I wanted a throw, she was always willing. At home, she didn't act like a nurse, that's for sure.

Sometimes, she convinced me to read a play out loud. "In the living room?" I said, "Just the two of us?"

"Why not? We can use different voices for each part. Come on, it'll be fun."

It wasn't exactly fun, but it passed the time. In bed, she'd tell me stories about the jungle. She'd signed up with the Peace Corps pretty soon after Kennedy started it, and found herself practically running a hospital out of a converted barn. "Believe me," she said. "You don't know desperation till you've seen what those people deal with. But some of them were a long way towards being self-sufficient by the time I left. And you've got a good head start on them."

Towards the end of September, some other nurses came over to our place for a party, all white stockings and starched blouses. A long-haired doctor came, too. Liz introduced me as her "live-in" and everyone nodded. They were all about her age, and after a little while I was feeling too old for them. I had another drink as they were starting to pull out the marijuana. I'd tried it once more since I'd moved in, and it made me sick. I decided it was time to take off.

"Liz, can I borrow your car?"

"Aren't you having fun? Have a hit. It won't be so bad this time."

"Yeah," said the doctor, who had his hands on a nurse's thigh. "Just get mellow, Jack." They had some of that hippie folk music playing on the Hi-Fi.

"I need to clear my head," I told her. "Where are the keys?"

She pointed to the table, and I snatched them. "I won't be long," I said. "It was good to meet all of you." I was really playing it up. I went to the door, and Liz followed me into the hall.

"What's wrong?" she said. "Don't you like my friends?"

"I like them just fine. I just feel out of place, where you're all so young, and have the hospital to talk about. I'm just going for a drive. Don't worry, I'm a very good driver." I kissed her and gave her a squeeze on the ass. Smoke blew into the hall, and she ducked back inside, looking doubtful.

It was after ten when I drove by the house in Dedham. The neighborhood was so quiet I felt nervous even driving by with that little putt-putt motor. I parked in front of a mom and pop store across from the high school and walked back.

It was a hot night for September. Voices from televisions and radios drifted out of open windows onto the street. But mostly the houses were dark, and no one knew I was there.

There was a cheap Buick in front of the house and a Cadillac in the driveway, both as dark as the windows of the house. Sound asleep. I looked around to make sure no one had gotten up for a late snack, and crossed the street. I walked up the steps to the yard, then onto the porch. In the quiet I could hear my heart pumping. If he had any bodyguards, I'd be dead inside a minute, but I had to see the best way in.

I slipped into the backyard. There was a small chain-link fence keeping a pile of brush at bay. A good place to hide when the time came. I crept onto the back porch and pressed my face against the door. I saw a back hallway and stairs leading up to the second floor. I thought of the attic and smiled. Then I hurried off the porch, careful not to make any noise, and kept walking away from the house. A good night's work. I took the long way around the block to the Volkswagen and went home.

When I got there, Liz had a fan blowing the smoke out through an open window. Her eyes were bloodshot, the way they always got when she'd been smoking. "Have a good ride?" she asked, but she hardly seemed to care. We went to bed and she started telling me about the party, but she fell asleep mid-sentence.

I hardly realized the time flying by. I got along with Liz pretty good, even with her hippie friends. The owner of the garage was a real prick, but I couldn't give up the job. As long as I was working, Liz let me stay with her rent-free, so I could save up for my business. She said it was a good investment to bet on me, and as long as she kept believing that, I had no reason to make waves. My real plan was, when I made enough to make my move, I'd set up a place out west, where no one would ever find me, take care of my unfinished business, and be out of there. In the meantime, all I had to do was show Liz my growing fortune once in a while, and I'd be off scot-free.

It went on like that for about three months. Winter set in. I had maybe six or seven hundred dollars saved up, but I figured I'd need about three times that to even consider moving on. I put up with the shit work at the garage, with the prick always bugging me to work faster. It seemed that every six weeks I had to relearn everything, with all the new models coming in, and all their new features. To keep up with it, I convinced Liz to swipe a few uppers from the pharmacy for me. Always good to have a few of those around.

At the same time I put up with all of Liz's idealistic shit about how great it would be for me to finally be reformed and my own boss. Sometimes, though, it seemed almost real, and I wondered if I really could do it. Forget about the past, build my own business, make a go of it. There were whole days when I didn't think about anything else. Then something would pop the bubble, maybe a newspaper story about another gangster talking to the Feds, and it all came back like a bullet into my brain. That woman took everything away from my father, away from me. I had to do it.

On Christmas, I helped Liz make a big dinner, turkey and everything, and she invited her usual friends from the hospital. The long-haired doctor was there, ready for the customary after-dinner smoke. I hated that part of the merriment, and so that's when I usually went for my rides. Today I was especially looking forward to it. I thought, it being a holiday, there'd be a good chance to see what kind of crowd the boss had around him, what I had to deal with.

Dinner was over, and they sat on the brown shag carpet around a candle shaped like Santa Claus, folk music on the

Hi-Fi. One of the nurses opened some wine, and they passed it around, drinking straight from the bottle.

I cleaned up the table, because if I didn't, the dirty dishes would be there for days before she had the chance to get to them. I'd already seen a roach or two scuttling through the garbage, a particularly nasty reminder of jail.

I'd just dumped the cranberry sauce in the pail and was about to scrape away some other leftovers when I heard Liz say, "No, not tonight."

"Why not?" said the doctor. "You just made a super dinner. Now it's time to mellow out. Ho, ho, ho, man." The others agreed, but Liz told them not to even light up, or they'd have to leave. "I don't feel so good," she said.

I looked out into the living room, and saw one of the other nurses take some wine and offer it to Liz. She refused that, too. The doctor looked at her a minute, then said, "Forget it, man. Let's find another scene. This chick's a drag." I couldn't believe this joker was a doctor.

He got up, and the others joined him. I came out and asked why they were leaving so soon. Liz just sat on the floor, ignoring everything, staring at the small tree we had in the corner. I felt like a goddamned husband who wanted to play bridge or something over martinis. But I really wanted my drive time.

"Sorry, George, man," he said. "We gotta split. Merry Christmas." They put on their coats and left.

I turned to Liz. "What was that all about?"

She was crying. "Nothing," she said.

"You have a fight or something?"

"No, I just didn't want to toke up, that's all."

"Since when do you pass up on that?" I needed an excuse to go to Dedham, but it didn't look good that I'd find one.

"I don't know," she said. "Sometimes."

"Are you sick? Too much turkey?"

She looked up at me. I must've been a sight, wearing an apron, because she started to laugh. "Oh, George, you'll make a hell of a father."

"What are you talking about?" I asked. I didn't like where that was leading.

"I'm pregnant, George. What do you think of that? I'm pregnant. I thought that would be a great Christmas present."

I blinked furiously, like that would change anything. "Am I the father?"

"Of course."

"What will you do? You can't have a baby."

She screwed up her eyes and stared me down. "Of course I can. Why not?"

"Your job. How're you going to work? Who'll take care of it?"

"I will. We'll just have to live on what you make. And don't call the baby *it*."

"I don't have enough saved up. How could you do this now? When are you going to have it?"

"In the summer," she said. "I think it's going to be a boy." She patted her belly and smiled.

I pushed my hand through my hair. "I can't believe you pulled this now."

"You think I did it on purpose? What, I can just decide when to have a baby?"

"Isn't it enough I'm here all the time? Now you try to trick me into marrying you?"

She looked like I'd slapped her, which was just as well, because that's exactly what I wanted to do. She knew I was in a bind. Whether the dough was for a garage, or a hideout somewhere far from Boston, I was in no position to leave. I needed that pile of cash, and the only way I could keep it was staying with her. Maybe she caught on I was planning on making a break. Either way, I knew it was deliberate. It had to be.

I took off the apron and got my coat. "Where are you going?" she asked.

"Out. I have to think. Where are the keys?" She handed them over, hardly looking at me. She was sobbing, but I could've cared less. "Clean up the mess in the kitchen," I said before the door slammed shut.

I drove around for hours, absolutely aimlessly. I should've planned on something like this. Why hadn't I? All the signs were there. She was getting older, and still not married. Us living together didn't give her the security she probably expected from me, and I should have known she'd want payback for putting me up rent-free. I must've been a fool to think she was doing it just to get me a new life. There had to be something in it for her, too.

I didn't know what to do. If I left, Liz could take care of herself. The most important thing was taking care of my mother. Everything else was secondary. No way was I going to let Liz get in the way of that, whether she had a kid or not. But if I left her now, I'd have to go through the expense of getting my own place, my own car, and by the time I was ready again to do the job, my mother would be dead of old age, and everything would be lost.

After driving all night, I went back to Liz. Strange, because it was a story my mother told me after my father had disappeared, just before I took Tommy out to the middle of Boston Harbor, that convinced me to do it.

Exhibit for the Prosecution

"Let me tell you about the Trojan prince, Hector," she says. "When the Greeks came to get Helen back, he had to choose between fighting for Troy or escaping with his wife and baby."

"Didn't he have to fight?" I say. "Wouldn't he a-been a coward for running away?"

"A coward leaves his family, and that's what Hector did. That's what your father did."

"No, mama, he loves us."

She flicks her hand, dismissing him. "Hector chose Troy, and left his bride and their son. He had one good battle, but it was all a waste. In front of everyone Achilles killed him, then dragged his body around the walls of the city. When Troy fell…"

"With the Trojan Horse?" I say. I remember that part from before.

"Shut up and listen," she says. "That doesn't matter here. When the city burned, the son of Achilles threw Hector's baby off the walls to keep him from growing up to avenge his father. The wife got sold into slavery."

"I don't like that story," I say. "Papa's not a coward."

"What do you know? Ah, if it was me, I'd have thrown the baby off myself. Better for everyone."

Chapter 28
Summer 1967

She told me that story to show what happens when a man turns his back on his family. Now I was going to be a father. Let her live, the old bitch. I was going to be a father. After all the misery I'd had over the years, Fate stepped in and let me roll the dice one more time. Old Snake Eyes was back.

I went back to Liz, and the next day dipped into the savings and bought her a ring.

We spent the winter getting ready for the baby. She gave up the pot altogether, and eventually those hippies from the hospital gave up on her. But Liz didn't even seem to notice. She was so caught up in this mothering thing she hardly cared about anything else. For some reason, the prick stopped riding my ass at the garage, and when I told him I was getting married, he gave me a raise. Just an extra five bucks a week, but it helped.

It was a cold winter, and Liz was always getting sick. She'd stay home for a lousy cold, so she wouldn't pass it on, and I ended up paying for stuff like groceries out of my savings.

"Don't worry," she said. "Once the baby comes and I get back to work, I promise, things will be great around here. You'll see. It'll all be worth it."

But things kept getting worse. In February, she caught an infection at the hospital. She got fevers every few hours that shot way up before they broke. Once, it got so bad she was about to go to the hospital around the corner, but it broke just before the deadline she'd set for herself.

"Good," she said. "I know the kind of care people get at those places. I'd hate to be admitted."

"Aren't you the one that gives the care?" I asked her.

"Sure. But it's like restaurants. Anyone who's worked in a kitchen knows what happens to food before it gets to the plate. You think a cook would ever eat at a restaurant?"

"Still, with the baby and all... "

"Don't worry, George, it'll be fine. I can tell."

But what really hurt was the money. Towards spring, Liz had to cut back on her hours so much that she was home more than she worked, until around the beginning of May, when she quit for good. She was as big as a house, and I was the only one bringing in cash. All my money went to food and rent, and my stash was getting smaller, too. I can't say I never thought about just leaving. At one point, I even had my bags packed. But I couldn't do it. Every time I thought, now's the time to make my break, something kept me from going. I actually wanted to see the baby, to hold him in my hands. I couldn't believe I'd changed so much. I bought a crib, and Liz laughed at me trying to put it together. "You can build a car from scratch," she said. "What's the problem here?" I laughed, too, and it felt good. But in all the old stories, when the hero got too comfortable and forgot his destiny, the gods always sent him a reminder to get him moving again.

There's nothing else to say. It wasn't meant to be. That last time I saw her, I realized how ridiculous I looked, thinking I could settle down like that. There was nothing more to be done, except one thing. I left the apartment, left her and the baby behind, and looked for a good car. I walked through the old neighborhood, where I'd spent almost my whole life, but I didn't see anything except potential getaway cars. I ducked into the movie theatre to wait until it got dark, then found the Delta 88 a couple of hours later.

I left that scene behind in the apartment, clutching my bag and old man's hat, and hustled up Cambridge Street. I saw what was left of my old home, what remained of the West End. The tenements were gone, nothing left of Scollay Square. Just a shitty wasteland leading to that new City Hall, dirt and cranes and bulldozers everywhere. Nothing left of my life with Tommy Costello, before he drowned, or with Stookie and Rose, the people I loved, the people I could've been happy with, if they'd only let me do what I wanted to do, instead of getting themselves in my way.

But now it was all turned to this fucking wasteland. Not even the ghosts of streets to imagine where I used to whip cars around corners delivering movie reels and then the Gang. Where I first met Max. I got to the Beacon Hill movie theater. They were showing a James Bond movie, *You Only Live Twice*. I liked the title, but I couldn't follow the story. Too many other things to think about, the horror I'd just seen, the horrors of the past, what I had to do to rid myself of this anger in the future.

It was dark out when I left the theater. I boosted the Delta 88 and drove to Dedham, and parked in the back of a public lot. I crossed the street to a small grocery store and bought some bread and mustard and went back to the car to make myself a bagful of sandwiches. Then I walked to my mother's house, the place I'd scouted so many times, with the bag under my shirt and my gun in my back pocket.

It was after nine o'clock when I got there. I looked around, then slipped into the backyard, into a little forest of bushes and trees. I found a few beer cans there, too, so I figured it was the place where kids hid from their parents. Fitting.

Around midnight, I crawled out of my hiding space. The neighborhood was absolutely silent. The main drag was a block away, and I hadn't heard a car in half an hour. I climbed up the back porch and tested the door. Locked, but with a cheap piece of shit. I picked it no problem, and that was never one of my strong points. Jesus, Mancini was an arrogant bastard.

The door opened on to a small mudroom, with a staircase leading upstairs to another landing. Nothing there except a couple of coats on hooks, and an electric washer and dryer. Hard to imagine that woman doing her own laundry. She must've had someone come in to do it.

I followed the stairs up to the attic. The door swung open easily. I flicked a penlight and saw a clear path to the front of the house, cutting through piles of junk on both sides. There were beds and tables and other pieces of furniture loaded with all kinds of crap. They had a fully decorated Christmas tree covered with a cloth in one corner. In another, one of those mannequins for making dresses. Probably belonged to the previous owners. I'm sure my mother hadn't done a stitch of work since my father died.

I walked past all the junk and through an empty doorway to the front of the house, which had nothing in it except a carpet covered with shoelaces. I couldn't figure it out. There were laces of every size and color, scattered all over the place like snakes, and not a single matching pair. Then I sat down on the rug. And I waited.

I leaned against the wall by the door, tying knots in the laces, trying to keep occupied. I ate a couple of sandwiches, and when I got tired, I popped a couple of reds to stay awake, pills I'd gotten through Liz. Her last contribution to my cause. When dawn came, I covered my eyes with my arm and let myself go to sleep.

I woke up late in the afternoon to the sound of a car door slamming. I peeked through the window and saw the two of them being driven away in their Cadillac. I ate another sandwich and tied more knots, waiting for them to come home. I pissed into an empty bottle.

They came back at eight. Maybe they had an early dinner. I heard the car drive away and looked out the window just in time to see the old woman walking up to the porch. I listened to them get ready for bed, listened to them talking about getting her another fur. I listened to them snore, and I almost laughed when I heard her moaning in her sleep, like she knew what was coming.

Then, the next night, last night, it was time. When I heard the car doors close, I watched from the attic window, saw it was just the two of them coming into the house. I put my hat on and stood up, cracking my knees. They'd gotten stiff after being stuck in that room of shoelaces for so long. It took a second to get my balance, but I was still closer to the second floor than they were.

I ran across the attic and down the stairs to the second floor. I checked the Python one last time, and kicked the door open. I was in a small sitting room, probably hers, filled with gaudy gold-colored furniture and leafy plants hanging from the ceiling. I almost ran into the huge television, skirted around it, and went down the hall. When I heard the key turning in the lock, I hid behind the door of another bedroom, and clicked the Python's safety off. The front door opened and closed, and the glare from an overhead light reached me. I listened to them puttering on the first floor. I saw Mancini hang her coat on a rack near the door. Then they started up the stairs. The time had come, and Fate was on my side.

I jumped out from behind the door and put him down like a dog. Then I did the same for her.

Chapter 30

Summer 1967

I don't tell Max about how she lied, about how she ripped open her dress, showed me what no son should remember seeing. Just the facts. And now it's all out, and I'm at peace.

Max whistles. "Next you'll tell me you don't like apple pie, neither. You mean to say all this was over your mother, that the old man got caught in the crossfire? They're starting a war over what you did, you know. A lot of men are going to die because of your notion of revenge." He helps me stand and step out of the tub. I'm woozy, but I can do it.

"Not revenge. Justice." I shrug. "Can't take the blame for all that," I say. "If it was meant to happen, it could just as easily been something else. I'm my own person, the rest is luck."

"Your own person, huh? And what's that broad Liz thinking right now?"

"We can leave her out of this, Max. She's nothing to me any more."

"Sounds like a good lay, at the least."

"Yeah," I say. "At the least."

We're not even out of the bathroom yet, and it seems like I've walked a mile. My arm is pounding, every beat of my heart a sledge against the stump.

"Well, you're right. She was keeping you back. But now you've got me. I won't leave you, pal."

"You're in it now, so you can't. You gotta help. First thing, like you said, get rid of that car. Then we need to move on. I'll be OK, if you give me your shirt."

"I can do better. I raided the doc's closet before we left. There's a couple of things on the bed. Your gun's on the nightstand. I'll be back in an hour."

Leaning against the bathroom door, I watch him go out into the dark. A minute later, the room floods with the glare of the headlights. Then the lights slip across the wall. I hear him shift gears and drive away.

Suddenly, I'm in total darkness and silence. This must be what it feels like to be in a pine box, I think. But then, when you're dead, you can't possibly hurt this much. I push off the door, fight back a wave of the dry heaves, and lurch to the bed. My mutilated arm feels like a pendulum as it swings. It sends a sharp pain up my bones, while the flesh around it throbs. How the hell am I going to get myself dressed without my goddamned right hand? My left hand has no idea how to work my belt, and it occurs to me that even when I get the fly undone, I can't bend my left knee to strip out of these wet and bloody pants.

Finally, the belt is loose. I pull it off and drop it on the bed. Now for the pants. I can't get the little silver hook out of its hole, and my right arm keeps trying to help and just gets in the way. I'd yank it off, but I can barely stand, and I can see my last manly act being a tug at my own pants before I crash to the ground, never to get up again. There must be a way to do something so fucking simple as taking off my pants.

Then I get an idea. I half walk, half hop to the closet and open the door. I feel around at about eye level, and bingo. Five or six wire hangers jingle in the silence. I grab one, and at least my left hand can work this one alone. Starting at the hook, I untwist the wire until I can feel a springy snake of metal trying to dance out of my grip. After it jumps a few times, spinning in my fist, I get it reasonably straight, then attach it to the outside waistband. Holding the inner part with my hand, I yank the wire with my teeth. Beautiful. That only took about ten minutes. Too bad I can't attach this thing to my stump.

But that's not going to happen. I use the wire to pull at the leg, until my pants are pooled at my ankles. All I have to do is step out of them. But it's not that easy. I can't lift my left leg, and if I lean to my right, I've got no hand to catch me. I try a few passes with the wire, but I can't make it work.

Then a car drives by the room. No lights. It passes the door, and now I can hear it idling at the end of the building. I stop diddling with my pants, struggle to keep my balance, barely breathing. A door slams, but the engine is still running. No other sound, but now instead of figuring how to get undressed, I wonder what the hell the goon will think when he opens the door and finds me with a wire hook in my hand and my pants down like a pervert in the shopping center. I gauge the distance to the nightstand and my gun, but with what might as well be shackles on my legs, I'd be dead before I could reach it.

I strain to hear what's going on outside. Nothing but the engine running. Who got out? Where did he go? Meanwhile, I stand here as defenseless as a kitten, with nothing but a length of crooked wire.

Wire with a hook on it. I'm a fucking idiot.

I can see the outlines of the furniture in the dark, see a white shirt on the bed, but nothing else. It should be enough. I fish the wire over the table, hear it click against the butt of the gun. Then I find the edge, and the trigger guard. After two tries, I hook it and pull.

The gun is too heavy for me to hope it won't bend the wire, but I lift it high enough that when it does drop, it doesn't reach the ground. It dangles like a trout, and I inch the wire up through my fingers until I can hold the gun under my right arm. Then it's a snap to grab it.

Now I'm armed, but I'm still a cripple standing in his underwear in the middle of the room. There's definitely someone outside. I see the shadow pass by the window once, twice. I hold the gun up, aiming as best I can at the door. I can get one shot off before I'm either dead or the recoil puts me down.

The gun is getting heavy fast. It was hard enough to stand before, but this is too much. Then the shadow passes the window again. Stops. Tries the door. I find the strength to hold my arm steady, start squeezing.

Then he's gone. A shadow passes the window and I hear the door in the next unit open and close. I wait at the ready another minute, until the couple hits the bed with a crash of a headboard against plaster. The walls are thin enough that I hear his quick panting, hear her low moans, hear his swearing and her shrill laugh when the pumping abruptly stops. If they knew who was listening, he'd never have gotten it up in the first place. And if I can hear them, what did she hear?

I put down the gun, wait until the john next door finishes trying to talk her out of her money. She stops laughing, and I'm certain he's the one that gets slapped. Then he's slinking past my window again, and his car drives off.

I hop to the bed and start getting dressed. It's slow, but I can bend my right knee just enough to hook on the pants Max left for me. The shirt slides on easily, except when the mass of bandages gets stuck in the cuff. The room lights up for a second as I yank it over the stump, but I can't give in to the pain. Now it's just a matter of getting my left fingers to work the buttons. I tell myself it's like practicing how to unhook a brassiere all over again. I did that when I was fifteen, I can do this now.

I have no watch, but it must be close to four. I learned the trick of always knowing what time it is. The drugs Doc Alsdale gave me might have screwed me up, but not that much. Besides, the sky's turning gray. The sun'll be up soon, and still no Max. What happens if he can't get back here? I'm a sitting duck, gun or no gun. But Max has never let me down, not yet, so I'll have to wait. Nothing else to do. And it's not like I'm not used to it. Fifteen years, I learned how to wait in the dark. Thirty years, I learned how to wait to avenge my father. One night, I can wait with my eyes closed. One night.

Chapter 31
Summer 1967

Gray light seeps through the motel room blinds. Another john's come and gone, and I'm guessing the whore in the next room is done for the night. I must've fallen asleep, though, I never heard anything over there. But what woke me up? Ah, it's my friend Max.

"Hey, Georgie," he says coming in. "Wake up, sleepyhead." He's silhouetted against the brightening sky, and one of his arms has grown. No, he's got a crutch. Good man, that Shiny Max. "Sorry I took so long. Thought I was being followed. Cops're cruising the whole state. We gotta move quick." He tosses me a paper bag. Doughnuts. "Eat up. You'll need the strength." He gives me a bottle of aspirin, too. I chew a few, then wash the bitterness down with another doughnut.

While I shove the breakfast into my mouth, he surveys the bathroom. "Jesus, you left a mess. We should leave the maid a good tip. It's gonna cost an arm and a leg to clean this." He turns to see my reaction.

"You spend all this time coming up with that line?" I say.

"Well, you've still got your health, right? Let's go." He helps me to my feet and gets the crutch under my arm.

When we get outside, I see that it's still dark out, but there's enough light to see outlines of buildings and trees. "Which is ours?" I say.

"That van over there." He points to a bakery delivery truck. It says, "Lupini's Bread and Pastries" on the side. "No one's gonna stop one of those this time of morning. And it'll let you stretch out."

"Good thinking." He opens the back doors, and a puff of flour escapes into the night. By turning and sitting on the bumper, I slide myself into the truck. It still smells of bread and pastries, and even though I'm not sure if I'm going to keep the doughnuts down, it makes me hungry.

"What've you been up to while I was gone?" Max says.

"Jerking off. Where were you?"

We're leaving the parking lot, and the bounce onto the street jars my arm. I swallow the scream, but the pain drowns out the first thing he says. But then I hear, "...so I left it by an abandoned train station with an empty case of beer. Made it look like kids on a joy ride burning up the evidence."

"There's been a rash of car fires tonight," I say.

"Too many on the road anyhow."

I angle my head so I can see Max and through the windshield. It's much brighter now. We're rolling smoothly down a tree-lined road, making good speed. "Where are we going?"

"You tell me, chief. Sky's the limit."

I think of my original plan. "Get on the turnpike. Head west into New York. Route 90 goes clear across the country. We can turn off anywhere we want after Chicago. Maybe play it safe and cross the Mississippi first."

"Works for me."

We roll on in silence for a while, each in his own thoughts. Finally, Max says, "So how many *did* you off tonight?"

"Couldn't say. Let's see, the old woman and her husband, of course. Then a couple of bodyguards back in Providence."

"And the one in the woods?"

"You heard about him?"

"Brother," says Max, "you're all over the police bands."

Who after that? Not Alice, but maybe one of those punks at the bar? And what about the police roadblocks? Just how big were those explosions? Max took care of the doctor himself. It's been a hell of a bloody night.

"Anyone else?" he says.

"No. No, that was it. I didn't kill anyone else." We drift into silence again. No, I didn't kill anyone else. Not me.

An orange ray of sunlight pierces the delivery van's window and lands on me. We've slowed down and turned off the road.

"What's going on?" I say to Max.

"Nothing," he says. "Just need to water the lawn. How about you?" But I've got nothing left to piss out. He follows a winding road, at least a half mile, it seems to me. Then he stops and says, "I'll be back in a minute. Hang tight."

The door slams and I'm alone in a cloud of flour. I think about the house where I lived with Papa and my mother, before it all went wrong. I can practically feel the heat of the bakery's ovens drifting up through the floor to my bedroom, hear the excited Italian murmuring of Papa and his friends, smell their cigars. I think that at any minute Tommy Costello is going to yell up to my window to come out and play.

How many did I kill tonight, Max wants to know? It started a long time before tonight.

Could it really be less than a week since it fell apart? Was it only Tuesday? Christ, it was so hot that day, and she seemed so tired when I left for work. "Go on," Liz said when I tried to make her something to eat. "I'll call you if anything comes up. Don't be late." Walking home, even with the breeze off the river, I was soaked with sweat by the time I got to the apartment. I could hardly breathe, it was so hot. My arms were covered in grease, and all I could think of was getting into the shower for a long, long time.

I got off the elevator and unlocked the door to the apartment. As soon as I walked in, I smelled something moist and sweet. I called out to Liz, but she didn't answer. Then I saw the stains on the floor, and finally recognized the stink. I called her again, and heard her make this ugly, moaning sound in the bathroom.

The door was open part way, but I couldn't force my way in at first. Her legs were stretched out against it. I pushed until I was able to squeeze through, and nearly got sick.

The puddle of blood covered the floor. Liz was passed out against the tub, one arm draped over the side. Her skirt was hiked up, drenched in blood that poured out of her. My first thought was she'd been shot. I took a step toward her, and my foot froze to the floor. She'd had the baby. Its head, blue and bloody, was almost lost in all that blood. The cord still dangled from its belly, but he wasn't moving. Yeah, it was a boy, my son, and I never saw him alive.

She looked at me. Her eyes had that same angry look I've seen on how many people, people that knew they had only a few seconds left. It was like she was blaming me for all this. That was all she needed to do to remind me happiness had never been in the cards for me. I forced myself to look away. I'll have that picture in my mind the rest of my life.

There was nothing more to be done. Fate stepped in and reminded me I had a job to do, that I'd been fooling myself all along. Getting control of my guts, I called the ambulance, packed a bag, and left the door open.

Now we're in a patch of woods. The sunlight flickers through tree branches waving in the breeze. I hear birds singing, and Max whistling as he pisses. I'm cold, though, and I wonder if it's the shade or if I'm in shock. No matter. I made it through the night, and in a couple of hours we'll put all of this behind. We'll find a place to hole up and get my strength back. I still have a chance to be happy, to start fresh, hand or no hand. Family or no family.

The Defense Rests

Max climbs back into the van. "All right," he says. "Let's get moving."

"Where are we?" I say.

"Near Worcester," he says. "We should get to the Pike in a few minutes. Comfortable?"

"Are you serious?"

He laughs. "Am I ever?"

We're quiet a while, then Max says, "Georgie, tell me. Did you really go through all this just to bump off the old lady?"

She looks at her husband's dead body. "How dare you?" she says. "I'm your mother."

"Yeah, just her."

"I gave you life. I gave birth to you."

"It had nothing to do with the boss?" says Max.

"No," I say. "He got in the way, is all. Why?"

"I'm just thinking, they don't know it was personal like that. You started a shit storm. They're talking about a war between Boston and New York. Maybe more than that."

"Who's talking about a war?"

He thinks a minute. "People. It's all over the radio, I told you. Did you take any cash before you left? Anything to keep you going?"

"No, nothing like that, Max. It was just a hit. Payback."

Then she shows me her shriveled tit. I point the gun at her.

He turns onto another road. My arm is throbbing. "Got any more aspirin?" I say.

"I can't stop just yet. I think this guy behind me's been close a little too long. Hang in there, pal. We're almost home free."

He makes a couple more turns. We must be in the middle of a town or something, going around the block.

"Between you and me," he says. "Who helped you?"

"No one. Just you. And I was damn lucky for that."

"Damn lucky," he agrees.

She looks at the body of her husband, then glares at me. "How dare you?" she says. And when she shows me that shriveled tit, she says, "I gave you life. I gave birth to you. But now I see I gave birth to a snake, a vicious fork-tongued snake."

Then I shoot her, right in the heart.

The van stops. "Damn lucky," Max says again. No other sound. He climbs out.

A second later, he opens the back doors. Light floods in and blinds me. When I can see, there's someone with him.

"What the fuck is this?" I say, as Max and the other guy reach in and lift me out. I'm struggling against them, but I've got nothing left. We're between a pair of warehouses, boxes and Dumpsters and wooden pallets scattered around. They haul me up on a loading dock, and someone opens a door.

"Good job, Max," says an old man. He helps the other guy lift me inside and Max follows.

"You fucking turncoat," I say. "What happened to loyalty? What happened to you? You were my friend."

Max pours the bottle of aspirin into my open mouth and I choke and sputter.

"Friend?" he says. "I was never your fucking friend. I'm your fucking conscience, that's what I am."

They drop me on the concrete floor, and my head cracks open. I feel the blood seeping out from behind my ear.

"Damn lucky he got to the boss like that. If I'd been on last night, he wouldn't have got close to the house."

"Yeah," says Max. "But you got him now."

"Let's lift him up," says the first guy, and the two of them grab me under the arms and toss me into an office chair. It tilts back with my weight and I can see them for the first time. I recognize them as Mancini's men. One has a scar on his cheek. The other one, the one who'd been waiting inside, has gray hair. The years haven't been good to him, but I think it's my father's old card buddy, Al.

"Who the hell you think you are?" he says. "Who're you working for?"

"No one," I say.

He looks at Max. "He say anything to you?"

Max shakes his head. "I think he's telling the truth. I tried every way I could to get him to talk."

"You're sure he trusts you?" says the old man. Yeah, it's Al. He was probably plotting against my father in my own house.

"Yeah," says Max. "We kept each other's secrets. Didn't we, Giorgio?"

I thought I had no strength left, but when he uses my real name, my head snaps up.

"How the fuck…?"

Max leans over me. "You think you ever fooled a god-damned soul with that hair dye trick? You think the old man never knew exactly where you were? When you washed up out of the water, Giorgio DiGiacomo, you should've just kept going. Your life would've been a damn sight better if you had. I never would've had to set you up like I did all those times."

"The night Vic Spruce got bit?"

"Yup."

"The bank?" I say.

"Like I said, a set up."

"What about the Statler?"

"Oh, that? I just wanted to pull a big score, and you were convenient." He smiles, like he just hit the trifecta.

"Got anything else to say to him?" old man Al says.

"No," says Max. "I did what you wanted. Now where's my money?"

No one answers. Instead, the younger guy lifts his hand. I see the gun and smile as he puts a bullet in Max's head. "Fuck you, you rat," I think as he hits the floor. At least there's some justice in this world.

"Next witness," Al says to me. "What've you got to say for yourself?"

"I wasn't after Mancini," I say. "He got in the way."

"You went there to kill an old lady? What kind of pussy are you?"

"She killed my father. It was a vendetta, and you know goddamned well I had to do it."

"Who'd you say your father was?"

"Rico DiGiacomo. He was boss. You knew him."

He nods his head in understanding. I'm gonna make it through this.

"He was gonna pass it on to me," I say. "She took it all away."

He shakes his head. "Now that's where you're wrong," he says.

"What?"

"He wasn't gonna give you shit."

"What?"

"Your father was the rat," he says in my ear. "Rico DiGia-como? He was ready to talk and ruin everything before we got it off the ground."

"No," I say. "He was the boss. He was gonna pass it on to me."

"Maybe, but he was going to blow it all to hell just the same. I killed him myself. What do you have to say to that?"

"Liar," I say. But something about it rings true.

"There are different kinds of friends," Papa says. "Someday, Tommy might move away, and you might move on to other friends. Just remember that family is always the most impor-tant. Always do what you can to protect your family, even if it means turning on your friends."

"OK, Papa." I'm starting to get sleepy again, and my stomach is churning with too many apples. What does that all mean? Why is he telling me this tonight?

Because he was cashing in.

The old man grunts. "The cops were putting the squeeze on him, and he didn't put up a fight. He'd gone soft, forgot about his friends. Rico DiGiacomo? He didn't have the balls to see his own dreams through. At least you showed some balls tonight." He pulls the bandages off my arm and slaps the stump with the back of his hand. I can't help screaming.

"Well?" he says to the other guy, the one with the scar. "What d'ya think? Let him off on account of the vendetta, or is he guilty of pushing the button on the boss?"

The kid deliberates a minute, rubbing his hand across the scar. Finally, he says, "He killed the boss."

"All right," says Al, the one who I should be killing right now. Rat or not, he killed my father. But he waves to someone I hadn't seen before, saying, "Get your ass over here."

Someone steps out of the shadows. It's a punk kid. No, older. Hard to tell in the dark. Maybe he's thirty years old, but his face has a familiar softness to it. And who does he look like? A dancer. Rose. Rose Kowalski, who I threw out of my apartment last time I saw her because she was going to have...

"This is it, kid," says the old man. "What you've been waiting for. You ready?"

My mother says, "I gave birth to a snake instead of..."

"Yeah," he says, and lifts the gun. "This is for my mother." Then, in the flash of the shot, I see it.

The shock of white hair.

"My son."

Made in the USA
San Bernardino, CA
15 December 2013